My Darkest Troubles

David John Vilfrance

ISBN 979-8-89130-355-3 (paperback)
ISBN 979-8-89130-356-0 (digital)

Copyright © 2023 by David John Vilfrance

All rights reserved. No part of this publication may be reproduced, distributed, or transmitted in any form or by any means, including photocopying, recording, or other electronic or mechanical methods without the prior written permission of the publisher. For permission requests, solicit the publisher via the address below.

Christian Faith Publishing
832 Park Avenue
Meadville, PA 16335
www.christianfaithpublishing.com

Printed in the United States of America

Acknowledgments

I want to thank the most important people involved in my life. If it wasn't for all of you, I wouldn't be here today—which also mean I wouldn't have been able to complete the book: Ivana Fleurissaint, Carmitude LaBranche, Edline LaBranche, Murlande LaBranche, Glana LaBranche, Gladys LaBranche, Alka LaBranche, Arnel Labranche, Gabriel Labranche, Alvin Labranche, Esther Labranche, Miralie labranche, Laura Saintilus, Lance Saintilus, Vanessa Vilfrance, Ivonna Vilfrance, and Jeanne Saintilus.

Love you.

CHAPTER 1

Why Am I Here?

Part 1
Damien

"Next stop, Whiting Street."

Exiting off bus 23, looking up the hill, he could see cars starting to pull into St. Barnabas Baptist Church's parking lot. With each step toward the church, the less willpower he felt to want to participate in today's choir service. As he entered through the double doors, the swift smell of myrrh entered his nostrils. Not wanting to be seen by the congregation's members, he quickly hurried into the choir rehearsal room. Having the room now to himself, he slowly walked from one end of the room to the other, when trying to clear his mind from what had been told by his pasture last week. Befuddled, Damien began to pace back and forth; he played back segments of the exchange of events that he considered moments of losing confidence. He eventually stopped walking and agreed to conceive his provocative thought, *Is life after death possible for a nonbeliever?* Hearing footsteps approaching, he prepared himself to greet members of the choir.

"Hey, Damien!" said Yemaya.

"Hey, bighead!" said Mary Alice.

"Aye Dee, what is going with you, bro? You weren't at the court the other day," said Sky looking at Damien, somewhat disappointed.

"Listen, everyone, we are running short on time, so let us rehearse for a few minutes before we head into the sanctuary," said Yemaya as she rested her purse on the back table. Everyone took their assigned spot within the formation of the group then Yemaya led while the group followed her hitting their notes to the song. "Wait, wait, stop. Who's off?" said Yemaya as she turned around to face us. From Damien's peripheral view, he could see Mary Ann's index finger pointing at him.

Yemaya asked, "You good?"

Damien replied, "Yeah, yeah. Let's go."

Yemaya leaned her head to tilt it so it positioned toward Damien's direction. As Damien continued struggling to sing on an A3 note, rather than continuing to make a fool of himself, he grabbed his backpack from the back table and leaves rehearsal. Walking down the crowded hall that appeared it could continue for days, the same question from last night troubled him. *Does life after death exist if...?* Twenty minutes before the service started, Yemaya abruptly grabbed Damien by hand and pulled him away from the crowd.

"We have to talk. Look at me. What's wrong?" Yemaya said.

Damien asked, "Listen, will you do me a favor?"

"What?"

"Tell Sky and Mary Ann I have an emergency."

"You think they will go to believe me?"

"Tell them that it's personal!"

"Personal? Are you sure you are okay?"

"Yes, I will catch up with you all at Thursday's rehearsal," Damien said while attempting to pass Yemaya, but she held his hand. He continued, "Yemaya, trust me. I will be okay."

Damien looked into her eyes, and then he slipped into the crowd. The church's clock on top of the sanctuary door showed 9:15 a.m., and the entire hallway was now crowded with new and existing attendees. Some of the people whom Damien recognized were chanting, "Praise the Lord. Thank you, Jesus," as they made their way into the sanctuary. As Damien made his way toward the front doors, an older couple bumped into him.

The older man said, "Sorry about that."

The older woman stated, "You old fool. Don't you know who that is? Put yo glasses on. It's Damien!"

He replied, "Wait a minute? Could that be you? Oh my god, it's you! How are you doing today?"

Damien exchanged handshakes with Mr. Thompson, then Damien hugged Mrs. Thompson.

Mr. Thompson asked, "Are you going to be singing today?"

"You sure did get taller since the last time I saw you, Damien," stated Mrs. Thompson.

Her husband replied, "That's because you keep shrinking."

"Naw, he bout six feet, ain't that right, darling?" declared Mrs. Thompson.

He said, "God bless her, please. She's suffering from that, whatchamacallit, Napoleon complex."

Damien said, "Mr. and Mrs. Thompson, it appears that service is about to start. You two should find yourselves a seat and enjoy the service!"

Damien politely excuses himself, walking some distance from the Thompsons, but he still manages to hear them going back and forth.

"Stop telling people that I'm four feet. I'm five feet five," remarked Mrs. Thompson.

He replied, "Jesus, Mary, and Joseph!"

As Damien slipped through the front doors, a sigh of relief began to settle in.

The sky had an enormous overcast, and pockets of puddles spread across the roads and sidewalks. The combination of a light wind and a drizzle caused the temperature to be slightly cooler than when Damien arrived earlier.

Damien threw on his hoodie, puts on his backpack, and walked toward the bus stop. While walking, Damien decided he won't go home; instead, he would go to the Museum of Brilliance and Creativity to reflect. As a kid, he lived in Charlestown, and sometimes on field trip days, he would visit the museum.

At the bus stop, Damien took cover underneath the roof of a building, and not too far from where he was standing, a careless older man was blowing his cigarette smoke in his direction. As Damien wiped some of the rain from his face, he could see bus number 23 approaching the bus stop. As the doors opened, Damien removed his MBTA pass to swipe across the toll machine, then after swiping, he headed toward the rear of the bus to find a window seat. There was no surprise to see anyone else on the bus except three or four people. Not too many people find the rain to be therapeutic, but Damien found it to be soothing, and at least for him, it helped to drown out the background noise. On the other hand, if the bus driver continued to hum church songs, it would defeat the whole purpose.

"Last stop, Ruggles Station Connection Orange Line and Commuter Rail."

Damien and the cigarette smoker stepped off the bus. Damien had to stop to adjust his backpack, and then the cigarette smoker tapped his chest. "Young man, can I bum you for a light?"

Damien shook his head and said, "I don't smoke!" Damien could see his train approaching the station from a distance, so he ran toward the toll booth, swiped his MBTA pass, then sat on one of the escalator handrails and slid down to the platform. Barely making it, he could catch the train before it shut the doors. Looking for a window seat, he found an empty seat not too far from where he was standing. Wiping the sweat, he laid his backpack on the seat next to him.

While staring out the window and looking at the track on the opposite side, he heard a buzzing sound. Damien realized that the sound was extremely close and vibrating through his backpack. After searching several compartments, he found the source of the vibration, which was his phone. Damien's first cell phone was a gift his mother got him for graduation. Underneath the word *Nokia*, Damien saw that he just received an incoming text from Yemaya. "The choir presentation went well, but people are worried. Can you talk?"

Damien quickly learns that texting can be challenging. Hitting the number 6 twice, then hitting it again three times, was a lot of work to type the word *no*! Finally, he patiently completed the words, "I will talk to you later."

Before Damien could put his phone back into his backpack, his phone vibrated, and it was Yemaya. This moment the text from her read, "Do you want to go to the Boston Common Park with me on Wednesday at 2:30 p.m.?"

How was she able to type all those words in such a short amount of time? he thought. Instead of trying to compete with her, he wrote "DK."

The phone vibrated again.

"Excuse me, sir," said an elderly lady sitting across from Damien.

"Yes, ma'am," he replied.

"What is that thing you keep playing with that keeps making noise?" said the elderly lady, looking even more curious at Damien's phone as it continued to vibrate on his hand.

"It's a cell phone!" Damien kept it short, believing there was no need to sound like an expert.

"Well, whatever you called, it sure doesn't look like it is bringing you joy," replied the old lady as she exited the train.

Damien happened to see two passengers across from him smiling and responded by simply shaking his head. He was not the only one who had been amazed by her cumbersome.

Next stop, Haymarket Connections Green Line and MBTA.

Damien exited the train and then walked over to the Green Line platform to catch the trolley. Not having to wait too long, he saw the word *Lechmere* written across the front of the tramcar. As it approached, Boston's basketball team's (Celtics) flag colors of green and white were painted all over the exterior of the trolley. Ask anyone who's not from Boston, and more than likely, they would agree that it is way too much green. As Damien stepped on board, he could feel his phone vibrating. He found a seat by the window then removed his backpack and laid it on his lap. His phone read: "2 unread messages from Yemaya." Damien clicked on the button close to where it said, "Read." "Please," she wrote, and underneath it, she added, "it would mean a lot to me."

He conceded and replied, "Okay."

"Next stop, Brilliance and Creativity Park/West End" was what Damien heard as broadcasted over the intercom. Now standing up and getting ready to depart the tramcar, Damien allowed being suc-cumbed while staring in awe at the beauty of the Charles River. The doors of the trolley opened, and the drizzle of the rain splashed across his face.

The feeling of calmness and some excitement saturated his mind and body. Descending the stairs, Damien arrived at the street-level floor on Leverett Circle. The rain and the wind began to pick up, with poor visibility, impairing Damien's eyesight. He managed to get to the crossing pole to push the pedestrian walk button. While waiting for the indicator signal on the opposite side of the street to change from "Don't walk" to "Walk," the speed of the rain and the wind flow both increased severely. Squinting, he could make out the word "Walk," blinking in white.

Not wasting any time, he quickly dashed to the other side of the street. While walking toward Charles River Dam Road, he thought about how he should've checked the weather forecast this morning before he left the house. From his head down to his socks and sneak-ers, everything was wet. After paying his admissions fee, he went into the restroom and sat on one of the bathroom stools. Undressing out of his wet clothes, he changed into his basketball attire that he was going to change into at last week's pull-up game with Sky. Using an air dryer to dry his sneakers, he finally felt light on his feet; he opened the door to walk over to the large mirror. While staring at himself, he thought about all the times he had put other people's needs before his, yet those same people rarely reciprocated the gesture. However, today was different, and Damien believed it. He felt good that he didn't have to make excuses about why he needed to stay at the church. Damien grabbed his backpack and looks at the mirror before saying, "This is who I am. No more hiding and no more lying.

Part 2
Tahra

The museum employee said, "Hey, Tahra?"

"Hey, girl," Tarah replied.

"Come here! Do you see that man over there?"

"Which one?"

"The weird one sitting on the chair by himself and staring out the freaking window! That one right there!"

"Hahaha. Stop it."

The museum employee said, "Maybe I should call security so they can keep an eye on him. Do you see what he has on, by the way? Why would someone wear that to the museum when outside it is looking like a tropical storm? Something is off about him, girl!"

Tahra replied, "Stop it. You know we can't be cracking jokes about our guests, and besides, we don't know if his wet clothes are in his backpack."

"True. Hey, Steve said he wants you to stop by his office before you clock out for lunch. Tahra Tahra Tee!"

Tahra had left her friend to get a closer view. Now standing only a few feet away, she began to observe the customer, whom she found to be uncommon but not in a negative way. From her observation, she could read by his demeanor that he was in deep thought; nevertheless, it did not stop her from wanting to intrude.

"Excuse me, sir?" said Tahra while observing his appearance. The man turned from the window to face her.

"Yes?" replied the young man.

"I just wanted to see if you are okay," replied Tahra paying close attention to how relaxed and comfortable he was looking into her eyes.

"Thank you, Tahra, for being concerned, but I'm good."

She was shocked and curious that he knew her name. He pointed to her name tag. "Right!" said Tahra as he smiled at her. "Well, I don't want to intrude. You did seem like you were in deep thought, but before I depart, can I ask you a question?" Tahra said, now moving closer to where the young man was standing.

"Sure," replied the man with curiosity filling his eyes.

"What is it about the Charles River that captures you?" asked Tahra, as she saw that her question had appeared to make an impression on him.

"Large bodies of water moving or small droplets of water falling, whether it's moving in a river or falling from the sky, either way,

I find it therapeutic," the stranger replied as Tahra caught his eyes traveling down various paths of her body, then rerouted back to her eyes. As he moved closer to stand in front of Tahra, he extended his hand toward her. "My apology. My name is Damien."

Part 3
Damien and Tahra

"How's it?" Tahra wondered how Damien's cappuccino tasted.

"Different, but I like it. The museum's in-house brand added the right amount of vanilla and milk, giving it a sweet and milky aftertaste. What about you?" replied Damien.

"Very rich! I'm sure you can smell it," said Tahra, while Damien smiled. "Can I ask you a sort of profound question?" asked Tahra as she prepared herself, tucking her hair behind her ears.

"Sure," Damien responded quickly, laying his cappuccino on the table.

"What is the difference between really existing and only appearing to exist?" said Tahra, now observing Damien's reaction. However, Damien was caught off guard but impressed. The last time he was asked a metaphysic question was by his teacher at Groton.

Damien said, "My friend James before he moved to San Diego with his parents had once told me that what is real is eternal, unable to be unchanged over time. All things that are absent of that attribute only appear to be authentic."

Tahra replied, "James would've fit well within my father's social club of idealism nerds. However, I can understand his logic, but I wonder what his reasons were."

"Something about being conscious of a…? How did he explain it to me? Gosh, it has been so long since he explained it to me. Oh yeah! If a person can see it, that person is of consciousness. Therefore, that substance or thing, call it whatever you may, is eternal."

"Do you believe that?"

"I don't know. Ever since I was a child, I only have been raised and trained to believe that Jesus is honest, and by confessing and believing that he is the Son of God, I will be able to see those that I genuinely care about in paradise."

"And now?"

Damien was silent, and Tahra was waiting for a response.

Damien stated, "Let's say that I was supposed to sing along with the choir members at church today, but instead, I'm here at the museum enjoying a fascinating conversation with you."

Tahra was trying desperately not to blush at this moment, but it was impossible for her not to.

Tahra asked, "Have you ever heard of the name Dr. Jean Dubois?"

Damien replied, "No. Who is he?"

"He's a theoretical physicist who also practices philosophical theism. This Wednesday, he will be at the Harvard University Sciences Center. You may gather a lot of insight from his presentation, as I always do."

Damien asked, "Oh, so you're going?"

"Maybe," Tahra replied.

"Okay."

"I'll be right back!" Damien watched Tahra leave the table and then go down the hall to get to the stairs; when she reached the bottom, she walked into one of the halls and disappeared. After waiting a couple of minutes, he finished his cappuccino and stood up, then walked over to one of the large windows that overlooked the Charles River and thought to himself, *Sometimes in life, it can be hard letting go of what you thought was real.*

As the rain slowly began to stop, Damien looked for a trash can to throw away both cappuccino cups. Walking over to the trash can, he felt a couple of taps on his back. "Excuse me, but where are you going with my cappuccino?" said Tahra holding what appears to be a pamphlet.

"Sorry. Here you go." Damien replied, giving Tahra her cappuccino. "I should be the one apologizing to you for keeping you waiting. I was looking all over the place for this. Here's the pamphlet with the address and time of Dr. Jean Dubois's lecture," said Tahra as she gave the pamphlet to Damien. Walking back toward the table, they both sat down, and when Damien unzipped his backpack, she saw some of his wet clothes.

Damien asked, "What's so funny?"

"You see that girl down there?" said Tahra.

"Which one?"

"The one in the blue shirt standing behind the information booth."

"Hmmm. Yeah, what about her?"

"She assumes that you came to the museum dressed in what you have on."

"What?"

"I know. I told her that you probably had to change your clothes."

Damien said while laughing, "Hey, look, I have to split. Do you want to walk with me to the exit doors?"

"Sure."

They both reached the exit doors, then Damien turned to face Tahra, and she looked into his eyes. "So I will see you at the lecture on Wednesday at 10:45 a.m.?" Damien asked, admiring her red hair while waiting for her response.

"Sure," Tahra replied.

"See ya, kid!" Damien said, throwing up the peace sign as he walked away toward the direction of the tramway.

As Tahra watched Damien walk away, she said, "Could it be because he's in a class by itself is why I find him so intriguing? I don't know, but Damien is holding something back. There's something he's not telling me."

CHAPTER 2

Time to Travel!

Part 1
Damien

It's Wednesday morning, and Damien rose out of bed. The clock read 7:07 a.m. He could hear the birds chirping outside by the tree, and when he pulled the curtains back, the sun and all its beauty illuminated his room. While heading to the kitchen, he read a sticky note on the kitchen door: *Your sister and I didn't want to wake you from your beauty sleep. We left early to run errands and pick up a few things at the swap meet. We'll be back by 1:00 a.m. Love you! -Mom.* Damien brushed his teeth and then took a shower. While getting dressed and talking to himself, making sure that he had everything he needed for today's journey—wallet, check; keys, check; and last but not least, gum—Damien saw the cologne that Yemaya purchased for his birthday last year. After spraying some of the cologne, he threw on a windbreaker jacket. He looked at the clock again, "And still got time to spare." Damien made sure that he didn't forget anything before he left. "Where's my backpack?" After finding his backpack, he threw a couple of pens and a notebook into his bag and headed for the door; as he walked out, his neighbor across the street waved at him.

Damien's neighbor greeted, "My man, good morning!"

Damien replied, "Good morning, sir."

"It's usually not normal for me to see you checking out the pad this early."

"Well, when I was a child, my father used to tell my sister and me that "Early is on time, on time is late, and late is unacceptable.""

"Okay, okay. I dig it. Your father is a wise man."

"I appreciate it, and I will tell him that."

"Aye, I and my ol' lady missed you at last Sunday's church service."

"Yeah, I was over by the Charles. I had an emergency to take care of, but I will be at church this Sunday."

Damien's neighbor said, "Damn. The weatherman sure fakes me out. That overcast doesn't look like it will bring positive vibes to anyone today."

Damien looked up at the sky and began to start shaking his head. He turned around to unlock the door and grabbed the umbrella hanging off the umbrella base stand. Before stepping back out, Damien thought for a couple of seconds to make sure he hadn't forgotten anything else that he might need. Damien saw his neighbor cleaning the small debris that was on his car. "Right on."

"Better I play it safe and take the umbrella," said Damien.

"Alright, man. I have to split."

"Peace out," Damien said as he walked to the bus stop on Talbot Avenue to wait for bus 23. As he waited for the bus, he thought about what discussions Dr. Dubois will narrow in on. "Son, are you okay?" A woman who looked to be in her forties observed Damien.

"Yeah, why?" replied Damien looking at her with a peculiar look.

"Oh, nothing. For a moment, I couldn't help but notice how you looked confused. I wouldn't worry about it. My husband always tells me that I…" she replied, but she did not finish her response as the bus driver opened the doors.

"What the hell was that?" Damien said as he followed her, climbing the stairs to board the bus. Damien observed where the lady would decide to sit so he could sit far from her. He found a corner window seat that was vacant which was ideal for him because where he was about to sit just a few rows behind the awkward lady.

The bus driver made frequent stops along the route until he arrived at the destination. Damien relaxed his head back against the chair, and while looking out the window, he thought about if he had three wishes and how he would use them. The first would be to travel to Judea in the year AD 32 so he could confirm if Jesus was authentic. "Ashmont, Red Line, Mattapan Trolley, and bus connection." Damien heard over the bus's intercom. Damien exited the bus and walked to the subway to catch the Red Line train. Removing one of his backpack arm straps from his shoulder, he swung his backpack to his front to retrieve his MBTA card to cross the turn rail. The train heading into downtown had not departed yet, and since time was at leisure, Damien, along with other passengers, boarded the train with ease. Damien found a seat next to the back by the window.

The conductor had just sounded off the bells to let all passengers know that the train doors would be closing shortly. Looking through the window, Damien could see more people making their way across the turn rail to try to board the train. The doors had closed, and the passengers had found their seats; Damien closed his eyes to allow his mind to drift away from the presence. What was once total blackness became a scenery of a mountainside desert terrain, and what had once been the sound of wheels screeching along the tracks was converted to the sound of heavy wind. Upon closer inspection, Damien could see what appeared to be a group of herders tending camels and goats.

"Hey, yo, yo, man? Are you alright?" Damien woke up from daydreaming, and while regaining his composure, he saw the eyes of some of the passengers staring directly at him.

"I saw you talking to yourself with eyes close," said a man beside him but was unable to make out what he said.

"What?" Damien replied.

"I said, I saw you talking to yourself, and you had your eyes closed. Aye, brother, that was like some Wes Craven weird shit. Are you sure you are okay?" asked the man looking shocked like the other passengers on the train.

"Next stop, Harvard Square." Damien heard over the train's intercom.

"Err, yeah," Damien quickly stood up and then made his way toward one of the exit doors. As he walked to the door, he lightly pushed his way through some of the passengers, and some of them were staring at him peculiarly. He was finally able to exit the train and to save face, Damien didn't bother to turn to look at the facial reactions of the passengers who were still on the train. Instead, Damien quickly moved through the people and hastily headed up the escalator. Once at the street level, witnessing how daily life continued made it easier for him to do the same. The traffic of the cars stopping and going and the fresh new faces of people either meeting with someone or separating from someone helped Damien realize that life carries on. Now moving with a bit of pep in his step, Damien heard his stomach growl. Not good!

Part 2
Nguyen

Damien asked, "Excuse me, sir. Where's the closest Dunks?"

This guy from Harvard replied, "Where is the closest *what*?"

"I'm sorry. I take it you're not from Boston?"

"Sorry, I just literally got here a week ago."

"Cool."

"So what is Dunks?" asked the Harvard guy.

Damien explained, "Dunks is short for Dunkin' Donuts."

"Alright, man, that slaps. I'm finna head that way, but you're welcome to join me if you want."

"Sure, man. Damien. It's nice to meet you."

"Nice to meet you too. My name is Nguyen."

"I'm sorry, but can you repeat it?"

The Harvard guy explained, "I know it's gnarly, Let me help you. To say the word, pretend we're talking in French, and you're trying to pronounce the word *Nous*. If you drop the letters *N* and *S*, then all that is left is *OU*. The second pronunciation of my name is *Gin*, like ginseng or ginger. Put both words together, then you have *Ou-Gin*."

Damien said, "That was good. You did a fantastic job breaking that down."

"Thanks. I learned from my elementary teacher, Sebastien, back in Vietnam."

"Okay. So, Nguyen, you're from Vietnam?"

"Not really."

Damien and Nguyen walked inside Dunkin' Donuts, and the atmosphere was loud and busy. They both walked up to the cashier, and Nguyen placed his order first. "Can I get bacon egg and cheese on a croissant and a large Peach Passion Fruit?"

The cashier then turned toward Damien. "And what can I get you, sweetie?"

"I will have an egg and cheese on a toasted cinnamon bagel. An iced chai latte, and instead of whole milk, do you have almond milk here?"

Damien was still looking at the menu, debating whether he should add anything else. "Yes, we do, love," the cashier replied, trying to get Damien's attention.

"Thanks, and please add three packets of sweet and low to that," Damien replied.

"What size? Small, medium, or large?" the cashier said, in a charming and alluring manner.

"Oh, sorry, a large, please!" Damien quickly replied.

"Hahaha, Jesus, Mary, and Joseph, are you always this well-mannered?" she said as she continued to laugh along with Nguyen and some of the customers behind them.

"You can credit my old man for that," Damien replied, feeling somewhat flustered.

"Well, I guess the apple doesn't fall far from the tree. That will be $18.80, love!" Damien reached for his wallet and pulled out a $20 bill.

"No way!" Nguyen said.

"Yeah, it's cool. No worries," replied Damien. With drinks and food on the tray, Damien and Nguyen surveyed the area for an empty table.

"Right here should do," said Nguyen, a table for two by the wall but not too far from the windows.

"So where are you from?" Damien asked, remembering the question.

Nguyen took a bite of his sandwich. "My mother, my sister, and I were born in Vietnam, but my Dad is from Los Angeles. During the war, my dad and mother hooked up, and then my sister and I were born. We're twins." Nguyen gulped his drink. At the same time, Damien carefully listened to Nguyen's story. "My mother told me when I was young that my dad always had difficulties assimilating into Vietnam's culture. She said he always regretted volunteering for the war, and so he had promised my mother that once the war was over, he would get visas for the family so we could leave for America. Once Dad got us our visas, we left Vietnam and landed in San Jose, California, and the rest was history," Nguyen replied, taking the last bite of his sandwich.

"That makes sense," Damien said as he chuckled.

"Which part?" Nguyen replied quickly.

"San Jose, California! Earlier, you said, 'Slaps' and 'Gnarly.' I played cool like I knew what you were talking about, but I got lost in translation," Damien replied jokingly.

"Hahaha." Nguyen shook his head. He asked, "So you hang out here in Cambridge?"

Damien replied, "No, I live in Dorchester. I'm here because there's a lecture at the Harvard University Science Center. Dr. Jean Dubois is the person who will be conducting the study."

"The physicist?"

"Yeah."

"I saw his name across the billboard in my dorm the other day."

"Really?"

"My roommate was juiced when she discovered that he would be lecturing on campus today," Nguyen said. Maybe what he was trying to say was that their roommate became excited when she discovered that Dr. Dubois would be on campus today.

"Wow! I only got twenty-five minutes left before the lecture began. Since you are more familiar with Harvard's Campus than I am, can you take me to the Science Center?"

"Yeah, of course. Let's go!"

Finally, the words *Science Center* above the building doors came into view. A lot of students were starting to make their way into the entrance. Nguyen looked down at his watch.

"What's the time?" Damien asked.

Nguyen replied, "Ten minutes before 10:45 a.m."

"Why don't you come?"

"Not right now, but I'll stop by later. Take my number down, man, and hit me whenever you pass through the area."

Damien pulled his cell phone from his book bag and put Nguyen's number into his phone. "See you, kid," he said as put his backpack on and followed a group of students into the building.

Part 3
Tahra

Tahra rushed into the building where she spotted a young lady at the informational desk.

"Excuse me," said Tahra, almost sounding out of breath.

"Yes," the young girl replied from behind the desk.

"Can you direct me to Hall C?" The young lady pulled a pen from her pin bin and a sheet of paper where she wrote the directions.

"Thank you," Tahra said as she walked toward the staircase, following a group of students who appeared to head toward the same place. Finally arriving at Hall C, Tahra proceeded through the double doors, where she surveyed how large the auditorium is. Looking down the rows, she didn't see Damien; she took a seat near the aisle to take a quick look at her watch.

"Ladies and gentlemen, we will begin shortly, so please take your seats!" said the announcer at the podium. Tahra stood up one more time, looking across the upper deck and then the lower deck but did not see him and so she sat down.

"Hey, Tahra! Tahra over here!" Tahra recognized Damien's voice but could not find his spot among the seats. As her eyes scrolled across the rows, she saw Damien's eyes locked on with hers, and she walked toward him.

"Hey."

Damien complimented her, "You look lovely."

"You don't look so bad yourself. Wow. It looks like a mini stadium in here."

"Good thing I was able to find you," Damien said.

"Ladies and gentlemen, please stand up if you can, and let's welcome and give a round of applause for Dr. Dubois." As the old lady stepped away from the podium, Dr. Dubois stepped on stage, and the entire place erupted into cheers. Jean began the lecture by asking philosophical questions, "Does reality exist, or is it only appearing to exist? Do you fully know? Can you confidently say there cannot be another version of you out somewhere in the cosmos?" Tahra looked at Damien, and she saw how attentive he was. While listening, his pen and notebook were out; every now and then, Damien would write something quickly onto his notepad. Tahra caught wind of his action and could see that Damien sincerely centered on Dr. Dubois's every word. "Some people subscribe to the idea that reality does not exist independently from the mind. That's to say, nothing exists unless it's perceived. To be is to be perceived. This form of philosophy is known as idealism.

"Then you have people who subscribe to an interpretation of quantum mechanics that there could be parallel worlds, parallel realities, and universes in an unnumbered amount of galaxies. It could mean it's pretty possible within these parallel worlds, there could be duplicate versions of you and me. Accept this as the many-worlds interpretation."

Tahra was taken aback by Dr. Dubois's explanation of "the many-worlds theory." The way he described it not only resonated with her views on life but also confirmed and supported her position as an agnostic. She glanced over at Damien and saw him drawing large pictures that connected to medium-sized clouds that had captions of notes within them.

Upon closer inspection, the images revealed a picture of four planets, then a picture of four suns, and then a view of four individuals with the number one labeled with the word "Original," and the remaining numbers that have been grouped are marked with the phrase "Duplicates." And above at the top header position of the paper was labeled in capital letters, "MANY-WORLDS INTERPRETATION."

"If you want to know more about our reality, then you have to attempt to understand quantum mechanics, which is a tool that we physicists use to help us discern the difference between what we see and what is. Suppose you find this fascinating and would like to know how it all works, you are welcome to come down and purchase a copy of my book on the shelf. Let me close this by saying I want to thank you all for attending today's lecture, and I hope I was able to unravel anyone's plans of living a protected life. Also, I want you to live a life of adventure and a love for chasing inquisitiveness. Good day to you all!" said Dr. Dubois as the entire auditorium stood up and cheered as they gave the doctor a round of applause.

"Whoa!" Tahra exclaimed.

Damien said, "Many-worlds interpretation!"

"I know. Look, he is taking questions. We should meet him."

"You sure?"

"Are you freaking kidding me? Yeah!" Tahra grabbed her purse, and Damien put his notebook into his bag and followed her down the stairs. Waiting in line along with the other guest staying to speak to the doctor, Tahra noticed something was off with Damien. Keeping a stealthy observation, they continued to wait to call next.

"Damien, Damien?" Tahra said and now reaching for Damien's shoulder, which startled him. "Are you okay?" asked Tahra.

"Yes, of course. Why?" Damien replied and could see Dr. Dubois staring at him along with a couple of other people within proximity.

"Hi, Dr. Dubois. My name is Tahra, and this is my friend, Damien," Tahra said as she saw Damien waving his hand at the doctor. "We enjoyed your lecture," Tara said as the doctor stepped closer to them and extended his hand toward her.

"Nice to meet you, Tahra, and thank you. Nice to meet you, Damien. How did you find my lecture?" asked the doctor, with Tahra noticing that the doctor appeared to examine Damien.

"I enjoyed the lecture. There were some points that you touched on that made me wonder, but overall, I was intrigued," responded Damien.

As more people came down to see the doctor, a circle of guests gathered around Tahra, Damien, and Dubois. As a result, Tahra began to see bubbles of sweat along Damien's face.

"Interesting. Which points I made did cause you to wonder?" said Doctor Dubois.

At this moment, Tahra saw Damien looking at the doctor like an alien from another planet. Then from her peripheral view, she could see several eyes locked on him. Tahra could see that Damien was sweating heavily. She then faced the crowd. "I came. I saw. I made it awkward." As laughter emitted from the public, she watched Damien breathe out a sigh of relief—knowing she was able to save his face from embarrassment. Damien turned and stared at Tahra while smiling at her. "Dr. Dubois, can I ask you a deep question?" Tahra stared at Damien in astonishment.

"Do you believe in Jesus Christ?" Immediately the people within the crowd became silent and now waiting for the doctor to respond to the question. "No," replied the doctor.

"Do you believe in the existence of a place called hell?" asked Damien.

"I do. I believe we all, at some point in our life, have experienced it. However, I don't subscribe to the belief that hell is a separate world in which the dead continues to exist," replied Dubois.

"I assume that you're a Christian?" the doctor asked. Tahra watched as Damien shifted his face toward Dubois.

"Not by choice," Damien replied as Tahra saw several people from the crowd nodding their heads in agreement.

"If it's not too personal, can you explain?" asked the doctor, looking more curious than before.

"Sure. Ever since I was a child, my mother forcefully made me believe that Jesus Christ is the Son of God. My mother, along with my pastor, would often repeat the scripture John 3:16 to me: *and that whoever believes in him shall not perish but have eternal life.* However, I never did stop having difficulties with subscribing to that belief," Damien replied as Tahra noticed Damien squinting into the crowd waving his hand at a man wearing a Harvard T-shirt.

"What did you find difficult regarding subscribing to that belief?" asked the young man in the crowd.

"I remember at the time asking myself, 'What are their reasons for constantly giving me this counsel?' Then one day, it came to me like an epiphany where I finally realized I did not have a choice. Perhaps I might've been pressured to choose—either be an enslaved person for Jesus Christ or be enslaved to my mind's consciousnesses," Damien replied.

"I want to thank you for sharing your story with us. I know most here can relate. If I may, I would like to share this with you and everyone here. Don't demand or look for security. Instead, demand and seek adventure. Better to live thirty years full of adventure than to live one hundred years in the corner. You see, it's not important how long you live; rather, what's important is how you live!" said Dr. Dubois. He shook Damien's hand, and the crowd gave a round of applause.

Part 4
Tahra and Damien

Damien and Tahra walked back to the subway station. Tahra asked Damien a question. "Damien?"

"Yeah?"

"Do you often regret helping the people closest to you?"

"All the time.

"How do you deal with it?

"I don't let them get too close," he replied.

As they boarded the Red Line, they found a window seat far from them. "Hey, you know when you ask Dr. Dubois if he believes in Jesus Christ?" asked Tahra.

Damien redirected his stare onto her eyes. "I do," replied Damien.

Not having the courage to continue to look him in the eyes, she stared out the window gazing out into the Charles. "My parents and I are agnostics," she said as she discontinued her gaze from the Charles River, only to focus on different parts of Damien's body.

"What's wrong?" Damien replied. Tahra hesitated for a couple of seconds.

"I don't know why I told you that," Tahra replied.

"Now entering Park Street. Change here for the Green Line" was spoken over the train's intercom.

"I guess this is us," Damien said. They both grabbed their belongings and proceeded to one of the exit doors. As they exited, she saw Damien smirking and smiling.

"What?" Tahra asked.

"Nothing, it's just I can't help but think that time moves more slowly when you're bored. On the other hand, it passes when you're with someone with good vibes," Damien replied while looking at her emerald eyes, and then his eyes would fall to focus on the curvature of her pink lips.

"Remember that life will not be measured by the number of breaths we take but by the moments that take our breath away," Tahra replied. Captivated by her response and her way of words, Damien's sexual attraction for her began to intensify to the point where he thought about crushing her lips with his, and so the longer she stood in front of him, the more it intensified. She smiled, tucking a few strands of her that overlapped her eyes behind her ears. The thought of kissing her lips was the sexual energy that seemed to invigorate him, but when he saw the clock by the stairs, which showed 2:20 p.m., a strikingly picturesque Yemaya began to appear before him as a vision. This mysterious revelation created a slight moment of awkwardness for him, which startled Tahra.

Meanwhile, Tahra was wondering why he was being so conservative. Then out of nowhere, Damien broke the ice and embraced Tahra with a passionate hug. As her face turned red, she returned the gesture before they went their separate ways. "You know where to find me if you want to talk or hang out, right?"

Damien said, "Of course." He smiled as Tahra smiled back. He continued, "I'll catch you later, kid!"

They turned around to go their separate ways. Damien turned around to look at her walking away, but of course, she didn't notice. He turned back around and headed toward the direction of the escalators. Tahra turned around to look at him, walking away, but of course, Damien didn't know. At the escalator, before he placed his hand on the handrail, Damien turned around. As Tahra saw the sign that displayed the direction of the Green Line, she turned around. Damien and Tahra stared at each other and then walked toward each other.

Tahra said, "I don't know what this means."

"I don't know either, so let's figure it out," said Damien.

"Okay."

After reaching into her purse, she grabbed her eyeliner and wrote her number on Damien's arm, saying, "You know how to call me if you want to talk?"

"Of course. 617-717…"

"Boy, you better stop." Damien pulled his cell phone out from his backpack. Tahra's face began to blush as she shook her head. She said, "You could've told me you had a cell phone."

"Nah. That would've ruined the moment. Catch you later, kid!"

Part 5
Damien and Yemaya

Damien went up the escalator, and while holding the rail, he thought, *I hope I can trust her.*

Once at street level, the park where he would meet Yemaya was across the street. As he entered the park, he couldn't help but notice how the area's landscape looked like a picnic picture from one of those Hallmark Cards at CVS. There weren't so many people in the park, which was ideal, but where he was supposed to meet Yemaya, there was hardly anyone there, and that was perfect. He saw Yemaya approaching, and as he squinted, he could see her wearing her black shades and carrying some small bags. As she got closer, he could see that Yemaya was wearing his favorite colors, a two-tone red, and a Black Boston Red Sox hat, along with a red top and black shorts.

"What's up, Dame?" Yemaya said. She walked up to him and hugged him. "Are you wearing that cologne I got you?" Yemaya said as she smiled. They both take a seat on the grass.

"Yeah, why?" Damien replied. "No, it's sweet, that's all, but you know how you left to service the other day. I was concerned. I mean, you didn't tell anyone why you were leaving." Damien stared at the grass and began to empathize with her.

"Yeah, I know. I'm sorry, I just had a lot on my mind," Damien said, feeling excited because he spotted his favorite candy snack, Nestle Buncha Crunch, in one of the small bags. In the other bag, he saw two tuna sandwiches and two Minute Maid Fruit Punch bottles. Damien kissed Yemaya on the cheek. Yemaya rearranged her body so she could face directly toward him.

"You want to talk about…?" Before she could complete her sentence, Damien outstretched his arms. His jacket sleeve lifted just a little bit revealing the black markings close to the palm of Damien's right arm. She zoomed in to get a better view. She turned to look Damien in the eyes.

Yemaya yelled, "Damien!"

Damien replied, "What the hell! What?"

"Why do you have a 617 area code phone number on your arm? Wait a minute, Damien? Is that eyeliner?"

Chapter 3.1

Heartbreak

Part 1
Yemaya

It's very windy outside today, and the birds that chirped away were no longer present in the park. Since the rain was striking from all different directions, some people began to seek shelter. As the clouds started to get darker, it was evident they could pour down at any moment. A small boy began to run around in the grass, holding his plane into the air while his mother chased behind him, trying desperately to get a hold of him; however, while showing off his excellent evasive skills, the little boy who was not paying attention collided into a man who has on a black T-shirt with the word *Dad* written on it. "Papa," the boy yelled out, smiling at his father. Then the parents, along with their son, became distracted by the commotion occurring not too far from them.

"Damien, you don't hear me? Now all of a sudden, you forgot how to speak?" Yemaya was demanding a response. "Let me ask you a question." She said to him as she moved in closer to him. "The person who wrote their number on your arm, who is she? Damn, Dee. Did you get dressed up for her?" Yemaya asked as she slapped Damien's drink out of his hand.

"I want to have a civilized conversation with you, but we can't have one if all you want to do is argue," Damien replied while maintaining his composure.

"Seriously, Damien? That ship has sailed, so you can miss me with that civilized crap and answer my question. Who is she?" Yemaya said as the look of being disgusted overwhelmed her demeanor toward him. Damien attempted to comfort her by trying to wrap his arm around her waist, but she rejected it swiftly.

"We should go," Damien said as he stood up and extended his hand to assist her, but she declined again. He looked down at her and could see that she looked depleted.

"I don't even know why I am mad at you," Yemaya said as she stood up with her back facing Damien.

Damien replied, "I find it interesting that you're demanding me to tell you this and tell you that." Yemaya did not respond. "Seriously, did you forget prom night?"

Yemaya remembered clearly, but she couldn't look at him in the eyes right now; yet, a flashback of the prom night replayed in her mind. She could see herself leaving the party while holding Damien's hand and Sky was holding Mary-Ann's hand, walking along the shoreside of the lake. That was when Damien confessed his feelings for her for the very first time. When Sky and Mary-Ann got their feet wet, it was at this point when Damien held her by the waist, stared into her eyes seductively, and then leaned into her ear and said, "You know, you have always been my crush ever since we were little."

Damien said, "Do you remember what you told me last year on that night? What was the word that you used to describe our thing? Damn, what was that word? Oh yeah, I remember now, *platonic*. *Platonic*, right?"

Yemaya began to sniffle, and after a couple of seconds, she felt Damien's arms around her; she now felt all of him pressed against her from behind. "I'm sorry," she heard Damien say to her calmly.

"I don't want to argue, Damien. Just tell me. Does it have anything to do with why you left Sunday's service early?" Yemaya asked, sounding calmer and less argumentative.

"Yes and no." She heard him say.

As the rain began to pour even harder, she turned around to face him. "I want you to tell me what happened when you left early during Sunday's service," she told him while glaring into his eyes. She grabbed a portion of his chin, and then slowly, she caressed both of his lips. "What happened when you left?" Yemaya asked, and while waiting for his response, he looked over her shoulders. The droplets from the rain begin to pick up. A couple who was sitting on one of the benches were holding hands and caressing each other.

"Okay, let us head over to that bench over there." She watched Damien point to an isolated, empty bench underneath a tree. Damien helped Yemaya gather her belongings, while she listened to him explain why he left last Sunday's service early. Before Sunday, Damien said that he and the pastor had crossed paths at church. He abruptly stopped talking and turned to look off into the distance.

"Can I trust you?" asked Damien.

"Yes."

He resumed the conversation, and Yemaya sat with her hands interlocked.

"I had asked the pastor if he had any free time on his schedule because I would like to talk to him about the faith of nonbelievers. He was confused by the question at first, but after a couple of seconds, he said the next day at 2:00 p.m. would be better for him to meet with me. So the next day, when I got to the church, I was surprised to see Sister Roberta from the counseling department. She escorted me to the pastor's chamber, where she sat me down on one of his couches. Then after five minutes, the pastor came into the room and sat down by his desk, then asked me what it is about the faith of nonbelievers that bothers me. I told the pastor that his last service about the lake of fire did not make sense to me anymore. I told him that after service, I left the church to find answers and reasons why it was just and fair. Then I remember you had said that if a person is ready to be saved, be rescued from the eternal fire, then they must announce Jesus Christ as their Lord and Savior."

Yemaya placed her hand on his lap, interrupting Damien. "That's correct, Damien. I don't understand why you are acting as if this is some new revelation to you." She shook her head in disbelief.

Damien explained, "I understand how you feel, but let me finish, please. So the pastor told me that is the truth, and that's the only way because God himself said it. So I asked the pastor, 'What about the indigenous tribes like the Sentinelese people who live in isolation from the outside world? Those people and similar indigenous tribes who remain isolated from the main society will never know Jesus. Will their souls get thrown into the lake of eternal fire?'"

After that statement, Yemaya created some distance between herself and Damien.

Damien continued, "The pastor leaned back in his chair and then turned his body so he could stare out of the window. He said to me, 'For God so loved the world that he gave his one and only Son, that whoever believes in him shall not perish but have eternal life.' I knew he had just given me an indirect response, and so I pulled my backpack from underneath the chair and grabbed my notebook. I was reading from my notes about the lake of fire from the Bible. I responded to him by saying, 'Furthermore, whoever that not found written in the Book of Life has to be hurled into the lake of fire.' He turned to face me and said, 'That's correct,' and so I asked him, 'Would Jesus Christ, Lord, and Savior kill a tribe of people who have no accessible way of ever knowing who and what he is?'"

Yemaya was shocked to find out what had been consuming Damien's mind; nevertheless, she continued to listen.

"The pastor said to me, 'He did it with the flood, and he did it with Sodom and Gomorrah, so yes. I believe he will.' We had to end our conversation because the pastor received a text saying somebody needed his presence. I left his chamber knowing that my conscious wouldn't accept his answer to be ethically fair and morally correct, and so last Sunday, when I stepped inside the church, I knew my synergy between the church and the people had been severed. I just couldn't be there, so I left. Outside the church standing in the rain, I wanted to go anywhere but the church—a location where I could relinquish the millions of questions that were running rampant in my head. While walking toward the bus stop, I remembered how my mother and father used to argue back at the apartment and, after several minutes, came looking for me and then found me somewhere sitting on the floor staring out at the Charlestown Harbor. I always knew that when times were not going well for me, the calm or turbulent waters seemed to reduce my anxiety, and that's why I went to the Museum of Brilliance and Creativity, where I could sit and process my thoughts and emotions while being across the Charles River."

Yemaya wondered why he had paused. "Don't stop. I'm listening."

So Damien continued, "While staring out the window, an employee did a welfare check on me."

Yemaya interrupted, "Why?"

"One of the staff saw me staring out the window for more than twenty minutes, so they started to get concerned."

"Cool. What is her name?"

"What?"

"You heard me."

"The lady who came to check on me?"

"Yes, that lady."

"Tahra."

Yemaya could feel her facial muscles tighten from biting her lip.

Damien said, "You know what? Let's forget about it."

"Why do you want to stop now?" asked Yemaya.

"Because you look upset."

"I'm not. I'm just hot, so continue." Yemaya could see that Damien was highly uncomfortable; nevertheless, that was the least of the things she was interested in.

"So I asked her if it was possible if life after death could exist if Jesus were not legitimate. But she didn't know the answer. Instead, she recommended that I see a well-known physicist named Dr. Jean Dubois. She said if anyone could answer that question, then it would be him, and so I took the pamphlet she gave to me. I just came back from his lecture today at the Harvard campus."

Yemaya asked, "What did he say?"

"You're not interested in that type of subject?"

"What type of subjects?"

"Philosophy and quantum mechanics."

"Did you find it intriguing?"

"Yeah, I did."

"So tell me. What did he say that you found interesting? Please wait a minute before you continue. I need you to answer this question. That girl, Tahra, was she there with you?"

Damien was silent.

"Seriously? Are you not going to answer me?" Yemaya said in frustration.

"She was there with me."

"That wasn't hard. Carry on!" Yemaya watched as Damien reached for his backpack and then pulled out his notebook. Yemaya looked at his notes with the words *Many Worlds* written at the top; unable to hold her anger anymore, Yemaya quickly stood up. The clouds were getting a little darker, and Damien could hear the thunder from a distance. She said, "How did you become so lost that your mind cannot distinguish between real and pure fantasy? Look at you. Do you even hear yourself? Do you not remember how you and the pastor would sit and talk for hours after Bible study had ended, and now you dare to doubt the man who has not only been preaching to us for eighteen years but also been like a stepfather to you and me? The same pastor told us on many occasions during service that everyone in the world will know who Jesus Christ is or will have the opportunity to know who he is. No matter where they are, people, wherever they are in the world, will have a chance to accept or reject him as their Lord and Savior."

Yemaya, now upset with Damien, grabbed her things.

Part 2
Damien

The clouds were getting gray, and the thunder was getting louder. Damien, still holding the notebook in his hand, pointed out to Yemaya the images he drew from Dr. Dubois's lecture.

"Wait a minute because I want to make sure I don't get it wrong. This girl you met at the museum brought you to see some physicist doctor who told you some mumbo jumbo about the possibility that more than one earth could exist. And he also said that there could be many versions of you and me in this universe," Yemaya said with sarcasm.

Damien didn't bother to reply but instead allowed himself to be distracted. As the wind carried the McDonald's bag across the park, it rolled in the direction of one of the couples he had seen earlier, now casually laughing and passionately caressing each other. The rain was now pouring heavily, and he could see the couple grabbing their things to leave.

"Look, I can't agree that I will keep your promise," Yemaya said while reaching for her purse.

"What the... What happens with, 'Yes, you can trust me'?" Damien said, looking at her in a state of disbelief.

"Don't look at me like that. Do you know you committed blasphemy by disbelieving Jesus's existence?" Yemaya said with tears streaming down her cheeks as she reached for her umbrella to stand up. "Look, I'm out." Yemaya walked away from the bench without saying goodbye, and Damien watched her until the frame of her body exited out of the park.

Damien was still seating on the bench, as the raindrops fell from the leaves to his head and face. As he leaned against the bench, still astonished at how Yemaya had just reacted, he heard an old man's voice.

"You need to get out of this rain before you catch pneumonia." An old man held an empty leash, and a small head of a dog popped out of the top of the man's coat.

"Thank you, sir! I will be on my way home soon," Damien said.

At that moment, Damien remembered when he was an eighth grader at Groton School. Ms. Callway had told him that rain couldn't give you pneumonia. However, not wanting to take a chance on it, Damien unzipped his book bag, grabbed his umbrella, then pushed the button on the handle. Moving quickly and trying to evade cars while crossing the streets, he realized the potential blowback he would receive when Yemaya would tell any church member. Not paying attention, a car almost hit him, but after trying to avoid hitting Damien, the driver nearly came close to colliding with a woman holding shopping bags. "Geez, what fuck is wrong with you, kid?

Sorry, ma'am, are you okay?" asked the driver as he stepped outside his car to assist the lady as he helped her to her feet.

Damien, now looking and feeling guilty, hasted his way into the Downtown Crossing subway station. Once inside, he retracted his umbrella, and then his heart began to murmur, followed by a sharp pain that pulsated throughout his chest. He leaned his back against the white-stained walls of the subway and proceeded to breathe in and out slowly. The pain in his chest began to subdue gradually.

Damien pulled out his wallet to retrieve his MBTA card and then swiped his card as he passes the subway's turnstile. Now waiting for the Red Line to arrive quickly, he noticed that the people and the images attached to the walls were becoming blurry. Something was wrong as Damien looked down at his hands, sweating all along his fingers. Damien touched his face and forehead, and he felt large amounts of sedation across his head and cheeks.

Damien was sweating profusely but didn't know why. He looked for a vacant spot on the bench, but they were all occupied. The smell of creosote from the woods on the tracks made him feel nauseous. Damien tilted his head back to stare at the fluorescent lights. *What is happening to me?* Damien could hear music in the background, so Damien chose to focus on the words and the melody of the song. While listening, Damien couldn't exactly make out what he was hearing, and it appeared to be multiple instruments and men singing in harmony.

"<u>Some people live their dreams. Some people close their eyes. Some people's destiny passes by. There are no guarantees. There are no alibis. That's how our love must be. Don't ask why.</u>"

Bright lights flickered on and off, then a loud horn came from something, gradually breaking and squealing toward him.

"What the hell are you doing? Do you have a death wish or something?" said a small petite mature woman who couldn't have been any taller than five feet. Embarrassed but clueless about what just happened, he could see a crowd of people had begun to encircle him.

"Should we alert the police?" a woman with long blond hair and a yellow raincoat said to someone peeking over her shoulder. Damien, now understanding the severity of the situation, slowly stood up. "Please don't do that. I'm okay," he told the crowd. However, the public did not buy it.

"Yo. Did you see that?" said a teenager wearing a Red Sox jacket with headphones hanging on his neck.

"I sure did. He was about to fall onto the tracks, but that short lady over there pulled his jacket so he wouldn't fall off the platform," said a young boy who could be between the ages of ten to thirteen years old. Still holding his mother's hand, the crowd zeroed in on the lady wearing a black leather coat the kid was pointing to using his other hand.

Because of the commotion, Damien missed his chance to board the train, and waiting for the next one to arrive wouldn't be a wise decision. While he picked up his backpack, he thought, *What if someone had already called the police? Then it would be only a matter of minutes before they would arrive.* "Excuse me, excuse me, please!" Damien yelled as he pushed himself through the crowd.

"Hey, where do you think you're going?" a woman behind Damien said. Despite her and the others around her yelling and asking critical questions, he continued to push through the horde of people. Finally, he arrived at the exit doors; he headed to the nearest corner to collect himself.

The rain was no longer pouring anymore, but it was still drizzling. Damien's heart was beating fast, but the chest pain was no longer an issue. He thought maybe the reason why his heartbeat was beating very fast was because it was entirely possible that the police could be searching for him. Deeply concerned, he wondered if he could still take the Red Line home. He thought to himself, *How else would I make it to the house?* Damien walked down a few blocks and then disappeared into an alley, where he went into his backpack and pulled out his do-rag. Damien's reversible jacket had a hoodie that he can wear in two ways, so he pulled the jacket out.

As he exited the alley, Damien walked into a department store.

"Excuse me, sir? Does the store have a fitting room?" Damien said to the store clerk.

"Yes, it's in the back," the store clerk who looked very dazzling said. Damien grabbed a Gatorade and a pair of denim jeans then laid the items on the counter.

"Are you not going to try them on first?" asked the store clerk looking surprised.

"I want to pay for these first," Damien replied, handing him two $20 bills and taking his change. "Back this way, right?" asked Damien. The store clerk nodded his head. Damien stepped into the fitting room and switched out of the jean he had on to the new ones he just bought. He then placed his backpack at the bottom of the shopping bag and his old jeans on top. As he walked out of the store, Damien decided to take a detour to get back home but made sure to stay undetected by the local authorities.

Having to use this sort of stealth mode approach to get home and feeling like a fugitive that's on the run did not ease his anxieties. As he approached the intersection, he found the Orange Line connector at an alternate Downtown Crossing Subway station on the other side of the street. After crossing the road, he took his MBTA to pass out of his wallet to have it ready for the turnstile; however, before he opened the subway door, he looked up at the sky to only see small traces of daylight radiating from the sun. "What a day!" he said to himself.

He looked to see if they were any security cameras in the boarding zone, but Damien could not find any. His nerves began to dissipate, and so he sat down on an empty bench to recollect his thoughts. Damien started to think about Yemaya and how furious she was. Damien was perplexed, and so he said to himself, "She wanted me to be transparent, but when I opened up to her, I did not receive empathy from her. Instead, she demeaned me." Damien realized now that being truthful with Yemaya only created more problems for him.

While talking to himself, he became distracted by a kid and an older man. The two held hands as they walked toward a bench not too far from him. The boy pulled the man's hand while pointing toward the tracks. "It's a dangerous son," the man said.

"Please, Papa!" yelled the boy. His father grabbed the boy by his waist and then lifted him into the air to place him on his shoulder.

The boy laughed and said, "I see it. It is coming, Papa."

Damien felt relieved because he could hear the train approaching "Next stop, Chinatown."

On the point of sitting down, calmness started to settle Damien's body. *No more feeling like a fugitive*, he thought as he removed his hoodie from his head. The train exited the tunnel, and the small boy ran to one of the windows to watch the cars traveling along the Mass Pike Highway. The train passed through several stops including Back Bay and Massachusetts Avenue.

Damien could hear his train stopping. The announcement over the intercom said, "Next stop, Ruggles Station. Doors will open on the left side."

Damien was completely shocked to see how dark it was outside. It had been several months since he had been on this side of the neighborhood, he thought. As the train departed, the colorful boy waved at him, smiling. Damien smiled and waved back and then proceeded to the bus terminal, where he will wait for bus 15 to arrive. Maybe the saying "Every passing minute is another chance to turn it all around" was true after all.

After stepping out of the bus, Damien took a shortcut through the open field to get to the house. Walking through the area, moments of him and his cousins as kids who used to play football and soccer during the summer flashed back. And when it was scorching, the kids would shoot each other with super-soaker water guns while the adults would grill barbecue.

Damien walked to the door and knocked, but there was no answer. He knocked on the door again but a little harder this time. "Who the hell is knocking at my door like the police?" said a man behind the door.

"It's me, Dad!" Damien replied.

Before the door opened, he quickly remembered that his do-rag was still on his head.

Part 3
Damien's Father and Damien

"Take that crap off your head!" said Damien's father as he hugged his son, but Damien didn't hug him back. "You alright?" He asked, but Damien did not respond. Instead, he walked past him to get to his room. The softness of his mattress was the only thing thought of after enduring this dreadful day.

"Is it that bad?" Damien's father asked.

Damien replied, "It's weird, Dad. I feel like I'm stuck in a time frame in a mind frame."

"Explain it to me."

"Every time I put the needs of others above my own needs, not only do I miss the mark, but I always get the short end of the stick."

"What happened?"

Damien explained, "I don't believe in Jesus Christ anymore, Dad. It's nothing new. I have been lying to Mom, you, and everyone at the church for a long time. You know, one thing I finally realized? No matter how much experience I may have with being untruthful, it never fills the empty void in my life. And so with that emptiness and shame that I had been carrying for so long, I decided to step in the direction of being completely transparent. And so I determined the best person I could be straightforward with is Yemaya, my best friend."

"That's good, son."

"No, Dad, it wasn't good."

"Well, that's new. Ever since the both of you were children, you have always been inseparable like white on rice."

"Dad, she judged me, ridiculed me, and told me I committed blasphemy. While attacking me, I thought, when did she become super religious? She never talks like that."

Damien's father watched as Damien shook his head in disbelief, but Damien's father saw a phone number written on Damien's arm. "Well, son, I want to tell you I understand you, and I know you intend to be honest with yourself and people. However, I must say that you're not being honest with yourself and with me."

Damien asked, "What? What are you saying to me? I've been honest with you this whole time!"

"I will tell you, but let me first explain why too much transparency can do more harm than good. Transparency is supposed to shine a light on the facts, and if it stands alone, then we can determine the *who*. However, we rarely find the answer that explains the *why*, which leads me to my question for you. Why do you think Yemaya overreacted?"

Damien immediately remembered the moment when Yemaya went from 0 to 100, then he looked toward his right arm, and after he looked at it, he saw his dad's eyes.

Damien's father said, "Let's talk about her tomorrow morning."

"Morning?"

"That's right. We are going fishing, so you get some rest."

"Alright. Good night." Before Damien left his room to go shower, he thought about the incident that took place at Downtown Crossing and thought about what his father had just said to him about transparency and wondered if he could be an exception. *Better not take any chances*, he thought.

CHAPTER 3.2

The Dream

"Whoa! What is this?" Damien said, shockingly surprised. Why couldn't Damien anchor his feet to the ground? As Damien tried to get into position to see what was underneath his feet, he started to experience vertigo. At this moment, Damien couldn't distinguish between up and down. On his right, there were blue and green tunnels, and on his left, there were red and purple tunnels. In front of him was a green and blue super-extraordinary planet with a gigantic rotating gold ring positioned awkwardly. Everything around him did not appear to be three-dimensional but rather a dimension within many dimensions.

Everything around him, including himself, was rotating in a carousel manner, but suddenly, Damien became distracted by something or someone that he couldn't see, but he could feel. Whatever it may be, it was slowly decreasing his rotational speed, and it was also correcting his body position so he can now float upright. Damien now realized there was some form of entity around, yet Damien was not afraid. On the contrary, Damien felt safe. As he looked down, he could now see more of the ring and more of the super planet, and then amazingly, he saw himself slowly being thrust toward one of the green tunnels.

Damien got closer and was now able to see the outer perimeter, these tunnels that are spinning in spiral motion could be wormholes. The closer he gets to the green wormhole, the more radiant the color becomes. Then abruptly, Damien felt the invisible force again. Still, this time, it was changing his position to where he was no longer upright but relatively flat on his stomach. Now hovering above the center of the wormhole, he felt something holding both his hands and legs. While looking into the green spiral of the unknown, everything inside of it seemed electrified.

At this moment, Damien turn his attention to the electrical shock waves pulsating in every direction his eyes allowed himself to see, and he began to wonder if it would be a problem. Without warning, Damien thrust into the wormhole. Moving at an incredible speed but not feeling the pace, he saw a golden aura surrounding his body and shielding him from the green shock bursts of energy; as a result, the explosion of green energy dissipates into small red, yellow, green, and blue traces of wavelength. Light from up ahead became brighter than the previous one. Damien realized it was morning, and he was now slowly descending onto the sidewalk of his old neighborhood. He turned around to look, and the wormhole was no longer there.

CHAPTER 4

The Bond

Part 1
Damien's Father

The toad-mating calls were coming from somewhere close to the stream. A slight breeze from the northwest direction was ruffling the leaves, yet the sounds of nature could not take away the tremendous luminous starry night. As a result, the sky burst with magical stillness. That's why the Swift River is one of the favorite fishing spots in Massachusetts of Damien's father. It's also a good spot for the two of them to talk about concerning matters. While Damien's father held two rods in one hand, he turned around, pointing his flashlight on his other hand toward Damien. "Are you okay back there? You seemed quiet," Damien's father asked.

Damien was trailing a few feet away and carrying the tackle box and the bait in one hand and a flashlight in the other hand. "Yeah, Dad. Why did you stop? Keep going," Damien replied.

Damien's father smiled and continued trekking along the trail and into a deeper part of the forest. He said, "Do you know Isabella loves to fish?"

Damien asked, "Isabella Garcia?"

"Yes, sir!"

"No way. She is too much of a prima donna."

"Well, that may be true. However, my eyes don't lie, and I saw her on the cover of Freshwater Life holding the new 1998 Shakespeare Ugly Stik Graphite fishing rod. Yep, I remember like it was yesterday. The title said, 'Not only can she act, but she can fish too.'"

"Well, I'm guilty of judging a book by its cover."

"Easier said than done, my son."

After that, they walked across the bridge to cross cascades. Damien's father found a good spot along the embankment to set up. "So who's the girl?"

Damien replied, "What?"

"C'mon, son. Are you still asleep? I'm talking about your secret admirer who wrote her number on your arm," Damien's father said as he cast his lure into the water and turned to look back at Damien. He saw him attaching live bait to the hook.

"Dad, I want to ask you a personal question."

"Okay. What is it?"

Damien cast his live bait away from his father's line and into the reservoir. He then found a clean spot for him to sit down.

"Why didn't you and Mom stay together?"

Damien's father heaved a long sigh. "You want the short or the extended version?"

"Dad, Last time I checked, we were not short on time."

"Alright, but I will tell you how it began, and why it ended."

"Cool."

Damien's father went to sit by Damien. "The very first time I saw your mother was at an apartment that I was renovating. While painting the living room, I heard the door open, and it was the property manager Bill and your mother holding you in her arms. After the tour and inspection, your mother was excited to move in, but Bill explained that it wouldn't be ready until Friday. Your mother wasn't thrilled to hear that, so I told Bill to give her the key. I only had two walls to complete, and it wouldn't be a problem to knock them out before the day was over. That was the day your mother smiled at me for the first time. You know, now and then, when I go through the family portrait album, and I see your mother's smiles, I look back to that day to relive that moment. When we started dating, let me tell you that I had the best times, and never have I ever loved another woman like I love your mother." He pulled back on the rod, believing he may have caught a fish.

"So what happened? Why did you two split?" asked Damien sounding confused.

"Although I love your mother, I don't think she could ever love me again. She had suffered too much hurt from her previous relationship with your father. Consequently, it would be challenging for her to show anyone else the same love she had once given him."

Part 2
Damien and Damien's Father Continued

"Pop, can I ask you a profound personal question?" inquired Damien.

Damien's father replied, "What you got for me, kid?"

"Have you thought about whether we are the only planet in the universe with human beings?"

Damien looked at him and could see that he was baffled by his question.

"Well, I can't call it. I can't tell you if our planet is the only planet within the universe that has human beings. Why did you ask?"

"So the other day, I went to see a physicist doctor who gave a lecture at Harvard about the existence of parallel worlds, parallel realities, and universes. It's called the many-worlds interpretation, and within each parallel universe, he explained the presence of duplicate versions of ourselves existing in any way, shape, or form within these parallel universes. The reason why I asked you this question is because another version of Mom within a parallel world would have considered you as her first love."

Because of the awkward silence, Damien looked at his father from his peripheral view and saw him motionless, gazing across the reservoir. Damien knew that when it came to topics about his mother and his love for her, he always had been oversentimental about it, so he decided to let the awkwardness run its course.

Damien's father said, "You got fish."

"What?"

"You got a fish on the line!" he exclaimed.

Damien noticed his rod with the bobber on it has sunk underneath the water. He stood up quickly and dropped the rod he had in his hand and quickly rushed to grab his other rod. Filled with so much excitement, he almost tripped over himself, but luckily, he was able to prevent himself from falling.

"Oh shoot, I got something big, and she's a feisty one," Damien shouted out. "Look at this. Just look at those colors on her, Pop!" Damien said as he held up a rainbow trout.

"She's a beauty," Damien's father replied.

"I know that, right? She's so fine I can kiss her right now," Damien said, and then he kissed the fish on its side. "Ewwww. She looks great, but she doesn't taste so good." Damien then asked as he watched his father pick up a stone from the dam and toss it across the River. "Pop, why aren't you fishing?"

"Let me ask you a question. What caused you to become interested in the many-worlds interpretation?" he asked as he picked up another stone from the ground.

"Pop, it's sort of a long story," Damien said, hoping that would be sufficient to deter him from wanting to know the answer; however, his father smiled and threw the stone across the river.

"Last time I check, it's one reason we come out here, right? You and I come out here to fish, and having deep conversations is the perfect way to kill two birds with one stone. Don't you agree?"

Damien sighed because his father always knew how to make valid points, especially at the right moments.

"I agree. Do you remember when I told you last night that I never did believe in Jesus Christ?" Damien asked and to which his father replied yes. "Well, two weeks ago, I requested a sit down with the pastor," Damien said but was interrupted.

"No, kid, don't tell me you share with the pastor your lack of faith in Jesus Christ?" Damien's father asked as he shook his head.

"Pop, let me finish! So I was in his chamber, and once the doors shut, I didn't hold back. I stared into his eyes and said to him, 'I'm having serious doubts about my faith in Christianity.' Of course, he was shocked, but I continued. I told him that I couldn't believe and understand how a merciful almighty God could send his creation—a creation that he carved out of his image—which is supposed to be love, yet he would cast those same people he loves into an eternal lake of fire. They chose not to accept Jesus Christ as their lord and savior. How is that morally right?" Damien spoke with passion as his father nodded in agreement. "Because that man gave me a half-witted response, I walked out of his chamber without saying goodbye to him. The following Sunday, I tried to save face and decided to go to church, but after five minutes of being there, I felt like I was only torturing myself. I hurried up out of that building and caught a bus and train to the Museum of Brilliance and Creativity."

"Way out there," said Damien's father.

"When a person needs to get away from whatever, nothing can stop them. My church, my sanctuary to recalibrate my thoughts, is anywhere I can see the river or ocean. That phone number you saw on my arm, well, it belongs to a girl named Tahra, who insisted I attend that lecture at Harvard."

Damien's father started rubbing his beard. "I see now and understand. Do you believe it? Do you believe that there's any truth to the Many-World's Interpretation?" asked Damien's father.

"My physics teacher, who is familiar with quantum mechanics, once believed that identity through time is a matter through one instance in your life standing concerning another instance where relation says that your future self shares psychological continuity with your past self," Damien replied.

"What does that mean, kid?" Damien's father asked and sounding very intrigued.

"It means that if there are multiple versions of you across the universes, then all versions of you from your past and your future will all share an intellectual connection. The situation in the many-worlds interpretation is the same concept except that now, more than one person can descend from a single previous person." Damien and his father both looked into the sky and watched the sunrise. "Do you understand now?" asked Damien, and his father nodded his head in agreement. "Let me ask you a question, Pop. Can you say wholeheartedly that you truly believe there could be no parallel versions of you out somewhere in the cosmos?" Damien looked at his father, deeply thinking about his question.

"I can't say that because it may be a parallel version of me somewhere in another parallel universe. However, I must ask you, kid. How does this relate to Jesus Christ?" Damien's father looked at him.

"That's a good question, Pop, and it's what I thought about last night before I went to bed. One of the many things that the human species have is its exquisiteness. Generally, most of us are to believe that no one within the entire universe shares your uniqueness, and as a result, that's what makes you exquisite. More often than not, we are taught at a very young age by our family or the church that God has done something that he has never done before, and that is form man out of clay and breathed life into man, which he supposedly became a living soul. The next thing God did after he created man has put him in the garden in the east to tend it, but when God saw that man was alone, he created a helper for him. Now let me stop here to raise a rhetorical question. If the slightest thought about the many-worlds interpretations could be conceivable, then you must ask yourself, how can Genesis's chapters 1:26–27 and 2:21–23 make logical and reasonable sense?" Damien's father smiled and patted Damien on his back, then started to pack their gear to get ready to head back to the car.

As Damien followed his dad behind him as they hiked along the trail, he asked him a question. "Hey, Pop? Do you believe in Jesus Christ?"

While loading the fishing gear into the car's trunk, he said, "You know, kid, I always found it difficult to subscribe to the belief of Jesus being real. However, I do believe that there's a God." Damien's father started the ignition and pulled out onto the road.

"Why?" Damien replied. "I can't explain it, and I don't know why, but for some reason, I always believe that there's a GOD." Damien's father lowered his side of the window and lit a cigarette.

"Do you think it may have started since you were a child?" Damien said, trying to pinpoint the origin of when he accepted the belief in a God.

"Sure. It's possible, kid. I never had the opportunity to grow up with both of my parents. When my brother and my sister were young, my mother sent us to go live with our grandmother. As we got older, our grandmother told us why our mother left us. This lover she was dating did not want my mother's children around." Damien's father took another drag from his cigarette.

"What about your father? Was my grandfather somewhat involved in your life?" Damien asked.

"I don't even know who my father is, but that is neither here nor there. I consider my grandmother both my mother and father. She truly did her best raising the three of us. In my childhood, we had the Jim Crow law, but thankfully, the laws in the South had changed. However, it was still difficult to get a good education. Unlike today, when it comes to education and equality, you guys have it much easier than compared to the sixties. So once I dropped out, I was forced to get an education from the school of hard knocks. Do you understand?"

Damien quickly replied, "Yes, sir."

"I couldn't contribute to making a difference by staying at home, so I was the oldest to help the family. At age thirteen, I started selling crack cocaine around the neighborhood, so I have been through a lot. Sometimes I forget how thankful I am to be here still, and at that moment, I remember my grandmother's words. Before my grandmother passed, she would say to me. 'Niles Walker, I want you always to remember that God is watching over you. I know this to be true because I asked God too.'" Niles flicked the cigarette onto the road and rolled the window up.

"That's why you always leave before Sunday's morning gospel choir!" Damien replied, but his father just smiled.

It was bright and still early, but no one appeared to be outside. Damien and his father grabbed their things and walked up a couple of steps to get to the front door; meanwhile, while his dad was looking for the door key, Damien wondered if Yemaya had spoken to anyone from church. "You know, on the way back home, I've been thinking about the question you asked me earlier."

"What question?" Damien quickly replied as he followed his father through the door.

"How can Genesis's chapters 1:26–27 and 2:21–23 make logical and reasonable sense? If the Bible is not real, people must reexamine their belief in God." When Damien set all the fishing gear on the floor, he started laughing. "Pop, that's precisely the thing I'm trying to figure out!"

Damien went to the bathroom and washed his face. "Kid, I may not know the answer, but I may know someone who does. I will call the person before the end of the day and get back to you."

Damien looked speechless but also thrilled; he gave his father a handshake. "Thanks, Pop." Damien followed his dad into the kitchen when he opened the refrigerator for a protein shake; upon opening the container, he remembered that he tossed his rainbow trout back into the water. "Pop, that rainbow trout would have been good on the grill and not back in the river." Damien took another gulp from the protein shake.

"Son, we will always have a limited amount of minutes, hours, days, months, and years to catch fish. However, the moments shared between a father and son will always be timeless."

CHAPTER 5

Qui Vivra Verra

Part 1
Damien

Damien woke up to the sound of the garbage truck compactor's hydraulic ram crushing the neighborhood waste. Damien looked at the clock on the dresser, which read, "Thursday, 7:27 a.m."

"Arghhhh, I have rehearsal at 10:30 a.m.," Damien said to himself. He got up from the bed to head to the bathroom, and the house phone rang. "Hello," Damien said while yawning.

"You could've told me you were going to stay at your dad's house last night," said the woman on the other end of the phone.

Damien's demeanor quickly changed. "Sorry, Mom, I forgot," he told her, waiting for her to bring up the confidential information he shared with Yemaya the other day.

"Well, okay then. Are you going to rehearsal this morning?" Damien's heart started beating faster.

"Yes, why are you asking?" Damien asked her as he walked to the living room and looked through the blinds. His father's Jaguar was gone.

"I want you to tell everyone that their performance was great last Sunday. Can you do that for me, son?" Damien felt relieved.

"Sure, Mom. I will let them know. I will see you tonight. Love you!" As he hung up the phone, he decided he needed to see Yemaya and check on her. Hopefully, she was not angry with him anymore. With his towel resting on his shoulder, he made his way to the shower. The sun was not entirely out because it was still early, but many people were on the road. Good thing he packed an extra protein shake.

While he was walking down the street sipping his shake, he thought about the person whom his father had said he was going to call after opening the front doors to the church and making his way to the rehearsal room. He walked in and saw the members of the choir singing in unison. "Take me to the cross, so I can find out where you are. Forgive me for my sins and heal me once again."

They all stopped singing when Sky came to greet Damien. "Ayo, man, where have you been?"

Before Damien could reply, the rest of the members followed behind Sky to greet me. "You good, bro?" said Mary Alice. Damien remained copacetic.

"Yeah, of course, so you guys are working on taking me to the cross?" Damien asked Sky and Mary Alice while his eyes scan the room.

"Yep, Yemaya thought it would be a good one to sing this Sunday," Mary Alice and Sky placed their hands on Damien's shoulders as they bring him toward the back of the room where the instruments are. Suddenly, Yemaya exited the restroom and walked toward the wastebasket to throw the paper towel she had in her hand. She grabbed what appeared to be a musical note and then stood by the window, looking down at her paper.

"Hey, Yemaya, look who's here!" said Sky, but Yemaya remained fixated on her musical note. Damien took notice of her hourglass-shaped figure as Yemaya was against the wall. Her highly saturated orange designer shirt and black denim jeans with orange topstitched lined up smoothly and effortlessly alongside her hips. While the light of lust flared in his gaze, at that moment, Damien could make out the letters J. C. marked on her earrings. There was no doubt that Yemaya was making her eye-candy presence known; at the same time, she was recognizing and praising Jesus Christ while she does it. Yemaya advanced to the center of the room and passed our musical notes to Damien, Sky, and Mary Alice. Everyone took their position, with Damien standing behind Yemaya.

"One, two, three. Take me to the cross, so I can get to where you are. Forgive me for my sins and heal me once again. Provide me with your love so that I can drift above." Yemaya looked at Mary Alice.

"Start at 'Take me to the cross.' Start at A3, and Sky, I want you to back her up at the end. I do not hear you hit that C3 note." Then Yemaya turned to look at Damien. "Are you even singing, or are you just standing there? I need you to support Mary and Sky throughout, so keep it at A3, then slowly extend it to A5 at the end." They continued to sing until they all felt confident it would work out for Sunday service.

Damien tried to move in to grab his backpack, but he felt a tap on his shoulder; at that instant, he envisioned Yemaya standing behind him, but instead, it was Sky and Mary Alice. "So what happened to you last Sunday?" Mary Alice said with her arms folded.

"Oh, I had an emergency to attend to." Damien quickly replied, but Mary Alice's eyebrows lifted.

"So what was the emergency?" Sky's facial expression appeared to agree with Mary Alice's question. Suddenly, Damien was at a real fork in the road. Should he disregard what his father had told him about being too transparent could cause more harm than good, or should he protect them from being hurt and avoid telling them the truth at all costs?

"I need to talk to you," said Yemaya with her eyes piercing into Damien.

"Okay, let us go to the park," Damien said while Mary Alice threw a light punch onto Yemaya's shoulder.

"Hey, we were in the middle of interrogating him! We almost had him, right, Sky?" Sky and Mary Alice laughed.

"Yeah, just a little bit longer, and he would've folded under questioning," Sky said to Mary Alice as they cackled among themselves.

"Don't worry. If he committed a crime, I would ensure he doesn't get away with it." Damien looked concerned as he watched Yemaya put her arms around the necks of Mary Alice and Sky while staring at Damien. Before they left, Damien gave a handshake to Sky, and then he stuck his tongue out at Mary Alice.

Part 2
Damien and Yemaya

As they walked toward the benches at the park, Damien intentionally slowed his pace so that he could have a better view of her curves. And after a careful inspection, Yemaya did not disappoint; she oozed sex appeal from every direction. At this point, she didn't even know how to increase his euphoria with her allure. As she was ready to take a seat, Damien drew his attention to the surface of her body as it glowed effortlessly whenever her skin made contact with the sun. "So what did you think of the song I chose?" she said as she crossed her legs.

"It's okay," Damien replied, but Yemaya's facial expression indicated that he stop lying.

"Alright, I notice you changed the words of the song. 'Take me to the cross?' Like, was that intended for me?" Damien asked, but Yemaya, with sarcasm, smirked at Damien and then tilted her head in the opposite direction.

"Maybe," she said, still not giving him any eye contact. Knowing that she was still upset, he decided to take steps that would de-escalate the situation, so he moved closer to her to grab hold of her hand, and at that instant, Yemaya quickly moved inches away from him.

"Listen, I know you're still mad at me, but I need to tell you something." Her light-hazel eyes connected with his eyes for two seconds before she detached them to focus on the swings. "I want to tell you, thank you. You could've shared what I told you, but you chose not to, so I wanted you to know that means a lot to me." He grabbed her hand, and she turned to look at him. "You mean a lot to me," Damien told Yemaya, and he could see that she was starting to loosen up. He watched her tuck her hair behind her ears. Her overflowing seductiveness increased his sexual desire.

"Damien, I want to know something?" He moved in closer to her.

"Sure. What's up?" he told her while every other second or two, his eyes would slowly disconnect from hers and connect to her puffy lips and then quickly return to her eyes.

"So are you telling me that all it took was for our pastor to preach about the lake of fire for you to question your faith?" Damien was stunned by the question since he was not expecting her to change the mood. It went from him lusting over her body to him searching for a way to become serious and focused.

"Yemaya, I believe that if Jesus Christ exists, and he's merciful, he wouldn't destroy the people supposedly made out of his image. Just think about it, if I was a father to our kids, and I had expressed nothing but the utmost unconditional love for them, no matter what crime they have committed, the last thing I would want to do as a result of punishment is to terminate their existence forever. I can't accept that our supposed father, who is supposed to be a merciful God, would punish his children in that way for not accepting Jesus Christ as Lord and Savior."

Yemaya put her head down between her knees for a couple of seconds; at that moment, a slight breeze blew through the park. She lifted her head and turned to him with her eyes red. "So are you saying we will not see each other in the next life?" Damien put his left arm across her neck, and she resisted, but he tried again, and he managed to wrap his arm around her to comfort her.

"Remember what I told you about the multiverse and how there could be many copies of you and me within the many universes?" She didn't say anything, but she nodded to agree with the fact she did remember. "If I am wrong, know that there will always be at least one version of me who would have to believe in Jesus Christ, so we can never be inseparable. However, if I should die today, and my life force is carried away to a place called paradise, then trust me when I say that I will be waiting for you." She rested her head against his chest, and Damien could feel his shirt get wet.

"What if you're wrong? What if all the multiple copies of you choose the exact path you did, and all the multiple copies of you never get to reunite with all the multiple copies of me? What if you find me, and I don't believe in Jesus, and you do?" Yemaya asked with small tears falling.

At that moment, the lyrics from "One More Night" by Phill Collins came to his mind.

"Like a river to the sea, I will always be with you. And if you sail away, I will follow you."

Damien reached for his backpack to grab his paper towels for Yemaya. "You know how we learn about spirits at our church?" She nodded her head again as she wiped her face. "When we die, our spirit exits our bodies and drifts into the spirit realm. The spiritual realm is blocked and separated by a force that we as humans may never be able to see or may never be able to know why. These two reasons are why we cannot communicate with spirits. However, I believe that just as we can communicate with people across the globe and with astronauts in outer space, I imagine that in the spirit world, we will be able to do the same but with the ability to reach spirits across the multi-universes."

She lifted her head slowly off his chest and looked into his eyes. "And after you have traversed across multiple universes to find me, what will you do when you don't find me?"

He looked down at her because he felt her trembling, so Damien reached out to interlock her small fingers, and with his other hand, he caressed the back of her head. "I won't be the only person searching the cosmos for you. There will be large finite copies of me searching across multiple universes for you too." At that very moment, Damien slowly laid his hands on Yemaya's face, and they embraced each other for the first time.

Part 3
Damien

As the sun began the set, Damien was seven houses away from his home. He was casually taking his time and allowing his mind to reflect on the euphoric moments of the kiss that he shared with Yemaya for the first time. Damien had been waiting for a long time to know what her lips felt and tasted like for years. She did not disappoint, he thought; the softness of her lips, along with the way she caressed her tongue onto his, only confirmed what he had always imagined the feeling could be. It was more than an average kiss from a couple who have known isolation for months. It brought about a sense of wanting to kiss her more.

"Hey, Damien!" yelled a neighbor.

"Oh hey, Miss Shirley." Damien looked at her clothes, and he chuckled at himself because of the bright colors she had on.

"Look at you! Why are you walking with a little pep in your step? What got you in such a good mood?"

Damien continued to smile; he didn't care about anyone seeing him in a state of bliss. "Not what but who, Miss Shirley!"

As Damien inserted his key, he could hear Miss Shirley laughing. "Oh really, well, do you care about informing your nosy friendly neighbor about who this person is?"

Damien laughed and looked at Miss Shirley. "Her name is Ms. Anonymous. Good night, Miss Shirley!" Damien made his way into the house and then into the living room entrance, where both his mother and his sister, along with the pastor and the pastor's wife, were sitting on the couch.

CHAPTER 6

Everyone Sees Noon
at His Doorstep

Part 1
Damien

"Good evening, Damien! We can see that Ms. Anonymous must have made a significant impression on you." The pastor's wife said, seated comfortably on the couch with everyone staring at Damien.

"Right, I mean, I guess. Did someone die?" Damien asked, looking for why the pastor and his wife were at the house. The pastor stood up from the couch and walked to meet him, and while doing so, he put his arms across Damien's shoulder.

"No, thank the Lord he did not send us here to report a death, but a church member, a matter of contention, recently advised me. Now I strongly believe that our heavenly Father wants us to do the Lord's work by involving the church this evening so we can quickly address the problem at hand."

Each word from the pastor caused Damien to sink even more into a slumbering state of temporary loss of equilibrium. "Damien, why are you showing a growing interest regarding this many-worlds theory and life after death, and why are you having a lack of faith in Jesus Christ?" Damien's mother told him while seating at the edge of the couch.

"I will be right back. I need some water," Damien quickly replied. Moving toward the kitchen, he could see from his peripheral that both his sister and her cat, Mickey, lying on her lap, were staring aggressively at him. After coming back from the kitchen and seeing everyone's eyes focused on him, at that moment, he felt an enormous amount of pressure on his chest, which made it difficult for him to concentrate and formulate a complete sentence. "Who... who told you?" Damien asked as he frowned at the pastor while waiting for his response.

"Son, are you not going to answer your mother's question?" The pastor replied as one speaking authoritatively.

Damien walked to the center of the room to meet the pastor where he was standing then Damien began to size him up. "I don't feel it's appropriate to interrogate me like this. Who are you to demand me to explain something personal to you? Did I miss the memo or something? Was I scheduled for a late-night church intervention? Well, I will tell you this, I'm not going to explain myself, not a single, tiny bit, not at all, and that goes for the rest of you," Damien said as if he was speaking from his troubled heart.

"That will do, young man! Now, let me explain what's going to happen to you. First, I am excluding you from your choir duties until further notice. Second, I require you to be present at the church's in-house counseling service. Sister Shirley will make sure the rehabilitation staff sees you. If you don't violate any of these terms and complete your sessions, I will sign off on your completion of therapy."

The pastor's wife spoke softly, "Hunny, you don't think that's being a little too harsh?"

Damien went back into the kitchen and grabbed a Gatorade before he went downstairs; he told his mother that he was going to his father's house.

"But, Damien, I cooked for you. Are you not hungry?" she said, and for a moment, she looked remorseful.

"I should've known that this day was bound to happen sooner or later. It was inevitable," Damien replied while he stared at everyone, but he said what he needed to say and made a start to the hallway, where he grabbed his mountain bike. He placed his Gatorade into the bottle compartment on his bike and then proceeded out the front door, slamming it on the way behind. As he inhaled in and slowly exhaled, at that moment, that feeling of being calm brought him the relief he desperately needed.

Damien looked at his watch, and it showed 11:27 p.m. The night was still young, and the weather was perfect. It was not too humid, and it was not too chilly. Thursday night football must have ended because many people were outside talking about how Drew Bledsoe and the Patriots' defense defeated the Giants. Damien caught a whiff of both charcoal and ribs.

As Damien brought his bike onto the sidewalk, he heard a man with a Trinidad accent. "Damien, da is yuh? Mama Yo is yuh! Whey yuh been?"

Damien recognized the man. He walked toward him to greet him, and as he came closer, he realized that it was his next-door neighbor Kevin. "I have been around. Why have you got the music so loud, man? Is that Calypso?" Damien asked while inspecting Kevin's enormous grill.

"Yes, I have fete going on, yuh understand?" Kevin asked to which Damien replied no. "*Fete* means to party with da loud music, and so yuh drink and eat until da wee hours of da morning."

Damien watched Kevin remove the lid from a Dutch oven. "Smells good. What is it?" Damien asked.

Kevin began to dance as he reacted to the nostalgia of the aroma of his food. "Dis here is the king of food what yuh call chicken Pelau and pigeon peas. Yuh looking skinny, boy. Here yuh try some of dis." Kevin pulled out a paper plate from the table next to the grill.

"Hold on, Kevin. I don't eat chicken!"

At that moment, the look that Kevin showed Damien was peculiar. "Wuh yuh nah eat meat?" Kevin asked shockingly. Damien shook his head as he looked at Kevin, happily smiling.

"The only meat my body can digest without getting sick is seafood, so I only eat a Pescatarian diet."

"Yuh say a word nah can't pronounce but meh say dis. Respect meh brethren, yuh could lead a horse to water, but yuh cannot make him drink it. Yuh understand?" Damien replied by nodding his head in agreement.

"You cannot force someone to do something if they don't want to do it. Thank you, Kevin. I needed to hear that, and thanks for offering me food," Damien said.

"Next time," Kevin said to Damien as they both gave each other a handshake and then Damien departed Kevin's yard and rode his bike up the street.

The street filled with cars and most of their trunks; Damien felt the shake from the subwoofers. Damien approached a downward slope; at his vantage point, he gazed at illuminated brake lights reflecting across the column of cars on each side of the sidewalk. There were so many aunties, uncles, grandparents, and grandchildren outside that there was no space to walk on the sidewalks. Some were dancing, laughing, and playing spades, while others were behind the grill talking about Tom Brady. Damien decided to ride his bike in the street; he could not dismiss the disparity between the joy of the people celebrating and the melancholy and dull mood he was currently feeling. At the stop sign, he thought tonight was supposed to end with him going to sleep reminiscing about that particular moment he shared with Yemaya and not riding his bike at midnight.

On the way to his destination, he thought it would be best to rest at the head start school he used to attend. Resting against the school fence and watching the cars ride by, he remembered how he and Yemaya would wait for each other by the entrance so they could enter the school together. Damien grabbed his Gatorade and took a couple of gulps before putting it back into his bottle container on his bike.

Leaning back against the fence, he started to reflect on the time when he first got baptized at the age of seven. Damien remembered asking why hasn't the feeling of divine intervention or something spectacular didn't awaken to a new euphoria caused by the supernatural being. Damien tried to visualize the moments before he converted to Christianity and how, as a young boy, Damien thought about what would happen to him after he died. He remembered knowing his father wouldn't have an answer for him and how much it didn't matter to ask his mother. She would only regurgitate the responses she grew up believing in her church; besides, she and her family needed to know that Jesus Christ was Lord and Savior on her island. More than likely, it can be considered a well-known reason his mother was such a devoted Christian, he thought. But, be that as it may, was she ever told about how Christopher Columbus, along with Catholic missionaries, traveled around the coastal and the inland of her country to Christianize, most of the island inhabitants?

He shook his head back and forth, realizing how those natives and those enslaved people gave just enough false and misleading information that they wouldn't bother to speculate; consequently, they were unaware that they had just been deceived and manipulated. Under the circumstances, Damien's mother and his ancestors were brainwashed by force, and in that event, mentally, their minds had to be enslaved, Damien suggested. He knew that it would only be a matter of time before he would eventually have to stop deceiving his mother. Damien looked at his watch and turned around to look at the spot in front of the school where he would wait for Yemaya, then he hopped on his bike and departed.

Finally, Damien made it into his room at his dad's house, and while his dad was sleeping, he made sure not to make any sound while he carefully laid his bike against the window. He turned on his night lamp to empty out his pockets onto the nightstand. At that moment, Damien noticed his cell phone and thought about Tahra. He grabbed it and lay on the bed, pondering whether he should call.

Damien dialed her number, and as the phone began to ring, Damien thought about the way she looked the last time Damien saw her at the train station. However, after his eyes landed on his night clock by the closet, Damien immediately hung up the phone. "A big mistake," he said to himself as he hung up the phone and removed his shirt, but before he could undress himself, the phone rang. "Hello?" Damien said in a whisper.

"Somebody just called here?" said the person, who sounded very suspicious and upset.

"Oh, yes, I'm sorry. I didn't notice how late it was. Good night!" Before Damien could hang up the phone, his father came storming into his room.

"Damien. Do you know what time it is? Why you got that phone ringing like an ambulance?"

Damien's father looked sleepy and upset. "Sorry, Pops. It won't happen again." Damien's father shook his head and then left the room. Damien looked at the phone and noticed that the call had not yet ended. "Hellooo?" Damien was still whispering. "It is me, Damien."

"Wow! Did I get you in trouble?" Damien could hear the friendly sarcasm in her voice.

"No. Ahh, I mean kind of. Sorry for calling you so late. I didn't realize the time until the phone started to ring," Damien said as he tiptoed to close his door.

"Has anyone ever told you that you sound different over the phone?" Tahra giggled. Damien replied and said no. "I didn't think you would call me," Tahra said.

Damien readjusted his head against his pillow. "Why?" Damien said, sounding curious.

"I was thinking, like before we went our separate ways, maybe I came off too strong. You know?" Damien knew what she was trying to say, but he wanted her to explain it more, so he lied.

"No, I don't." Tahra sighed, and Damien smiled.

"Never mind. It was stupid for me to bring it up." Damien tapped the volume button on the phone to decrease the volume.

"I don't think it's stupid, and I like listening to you." Damien wished he could see Tahra's facial expression right now.

"You're just saying that so I won't feel bad," Tahra said.

"I got screamed at by my father while trying to reach you after midnight. I'm saying that. Doesn't that mean something to you?" Damien said as he took off his sneakers.

"Good call. Let me ask you something. Have you ever heard of the word *serendipity*?" Tahra asked.

"Nope, why?" Damien replied.

"Never mind. Forget it. It's stupid," Tahra said.

"C'mon. You got me curious now," Damien said.

Tahra said, "When we went our separate ways, I felt like I would never see you again, and I remember saying to myself, "That would suck." And so when I turned around, I was hoping that you would be standing there waiting for me so you could call out to me, but I was wrong. Instead, I saw you walking away from me toward the escalators. At that moment, I said that maybe it wasn't meant to be then, so I turned back to walk toward the stairs on the other side. Before I could go down the stairs, someone bumped into me, and when I turned around, instead of seeing the person that ran into me, I saw you looking at me."

"So that's what it's called?" Damien said.

"What are you trying to say? Did you experience something similar?" Tahra asked.

Damien replied, "I think so."

"Well, are you going to tell me?" Tahra asked again.

"Ummm, no," Damien said.

Tahra exclaimed, "What?"

Damien was trying hard not to laugh. "I was only joking. I don't remember how many times I turned around to see if you were looking at me, but every time I did, you walked away from me when I got to the escalators. I felt something that just told me to take another look, and when I did, I saw you turn to face me, and the rest was history. I saw you blushing as you walked toward me."

Tahra said, "Okay, so you do have a good memory. The meaning of *serendipity* has been interpreted as good luck in finding valuable things unintentionally, for example, in a fairy tale of a man and a woman always making discoveries through chance. You can thank fate for that."

Damien asked, "Sort of like how we reconnected back on the subway platform?"

"Yes," replied Tahra.

Damien said, "So what are you implying, Tahra? That your faith, my faith, may not have been planned. Because it had become so the moment it occurred. It became intended for you and me."

Tahra replied, "I couldn't have said it any better!"

Damien asked, "How do you do that?"

"Do what?" Tahra inquired.

Damien said, "The way you think and your choice of words always intrigued me."

"I will tell you if you first tell me what made you decide to call me after midnight," Tahra replied.

Damien said, "Okay, that was cute. I'll give you that one. My pops thought it would be a good idea for me to talk to his good friend about my interest in life after death, and so I just wanted to know if you would be interested in accompanying me if she decides that it's okay for me to come over?"

Tahra replied, "Life after death? Never mind, when are you going?"

"I'm going to try to go over there tomorrow. Is that too soon for you?"

"No, I will be at the house. Can I ask you a question?"

"About life after death?"

Tahra said, "No, not about that. I sensed that there's something else that you wanted to talk to me about that was on your mind."

Damien felt his gut turn because he didn't want to lie to Tahra, but he wasn't ready to bring up Yemaya at this time, so he lied to her again. "It's the truth. I just feel like she would be more relaxed and open with me if I were to have a woman with me, and I want you to be that woman." Damien was passionate in his response to Tahra.

Tahra replied, "Okay. Just let me know when you want me."

"I will let you know. Sleep well, Tahra."

"You do the same, Damien."

Damien hung up the phone, then adjusted his head to the softest part of his pillow and thought again of her choice of words that she said to him at the end. "Just let me know when you want me."

Dream 2

The entire sky was covered in deep dark clouds, and it seemed like every couple of seconds, lightning was piercing through it. Hovering onto the ground, Damien can see many people—including children—outside, standing against the building and using it as a shelter to protect themselves from the elements. Upon further inspection, he can see the children's frail, innocent bodies being shaken with terror as another thunder rang louder than the previous one. Deeply stunned, his mouth dropped open in disbelief as Damien watched the kids crying while each kid clutched someone beside them. He immediately attempted to walk in their direction, but something frightening happened.

Damien was no longer using his feet. Strangely, Damien could read and see the minds of people in front of him. He tried to get his focus on the girl with a pink Winnie the Pooh sweater. He started to hover over her. "Hey, what is going on?" Damien said to her, but not only did she not respond, but she also had no idea that a man *was* standing in front of her. The little girl did not attempt to make a single eye contact with me. "Hey, can anybody hear me? I'm your neighbor. I stay upstairs in this building here at apartment 3C. Hello?" Damien said, yelling and waving both of his hands in front of everyone's faces to get their attention, but there was not a single response or a single reaction from anyone. *What the hell is going on here?* Damien thought to himself. He departed from that group of people and turned his attention toward a young man approximately around his age standing against the wall on the opposite end. Damien tried to focus on what the guy was thinking. Damien hovered over to him, and upon further checking, Damien could see that the young man was looking petrified as the guy pointed to the sky. "What the heck was he looking at up there? Oh sh——!"

CHAPTER 7

One Nail Drive Out Another

Part 1
Damien

He woke up to the smell of bacon; the scent of pork from the kitchen only confirmed that his father was cooking something big and heavy. He looked toward the closet and saw that the time on the clock was still early, and because he didn't get a total of eight hours of sleep, it was a struggle between sleep and willpower. For that reason, he managed to slowly crawl out of his bed where he reached out for his towel that was hanging off the top of his door. "There you are. You want some?" Damien saw his father making himself a plate with eggs, grits, bacon, and a biscuit.

"Sure, but don't add any of that pork to my plate," Damien said while walking toward the refrigerator to grab some orange juice.

"Do I need to get used to hearing your phone going off around midnight?" Damien's father said raising one of his eyebrows.

"That's my fault, Pop, and it won't happen again," Damien said as he passed his father to get to one of the shelves to grab a cup.

"Well, you're not the only one here whose phone rang after midnight." Damien looked at his father, confused. "Your mother called while you were in bed." Damien looked at his plate and took a bite from the eggs.

"Oh yeah. What did she say?" Damien replied but was not surprised that she called.

"She wouldn't tell me. She just said that she needed to talk to you, but when I went into your room, and I saw you snoring like a baby, I told her no and that I would have you call her when you get up, then she hung up on me." Damien chuckled, and then his father chuckled, and they both laughed.

"Alright. I'll take your advice and see if your friend can meet with me today." Damien saw his father take a big bite from the bacon. "Yuck," Damien said.

"I would be surprised if she could squeeze you in today," Damien's father said as he finished his plate.

"Maybe you're right, or maybe she might make an exception for me once she realizes that it's her close friend's son who's asking," Damien said as he smiled and winked at his father.

*****

"Hello, can I please speak to Ms. Nolan?" Damien said to the person who has a soft, pleasant foreign accent.

"Yes, lad," Damien immediately sat up from his bed.

"Ms. Nolan, my name is Damien, Niles Walker's son." Damien heard the sound of a tea kettle screaming in the background for a couple of seconds.

"Oh ya, ha-ware-ya?"

Damien smiled. "I'm okay, thanks for asking, Ms. Nolan, I know you and my father have spoken about me scheduling a time to meet with you." Damien stood up from his bed and headed toward the window. "I was hoping you would be free to meet with me today?" Damien said as he looked at the mist of fog and drizzle blanketing the neighborhood.

"Well, it's raining, but if you don't mind getting wet, I don't mind having you as my guest," Ms. Nolan said as the sound of a tea kettle pot poured into something.

"Is it okay to bring my friend Tahra?" Damien waited patiently for her response as there was an awkward silence.

"Is it okay to bring my girlfriend?"

Damien was flabbergasted. "Sure, Ms. Nolan. We would be pleased if she could accompany you." Damien replied as he searched for clothes to wear.

"Grand. Take me address down." Damien grabbed his backpack and pulled out a pen.

"Okay. I will call you if I get lost," Damien said as he pulled out his Timberland boots from his closet.

"Right. We will have something prepared when you get here. See you soon!"

*****

"Hey, Tahra," greeted Damien.

Tahra replied, "Good morning."

"Sorry. Good morning. Can you meet me at Downtown Crossing at…11:30 a.m.?"

There was no response from Tahra.

Damien asked, "Hey, are you well?"

"Yeah, just deciding what to wear, but I should be there around that time. Are you going to be waiting at the Red Line or Orange Line platform?"

"Not the Red Line. She lives in Charlestown, so meet me on the Orange Line platform," he said. He could hear doors opening and closing.

"Wow! It has been years since I visited Charlestown. Well, alright, I'll see you soon."

"Wait! Please tell me what you will wear so I can spot you."

"What do you want me to wear?"

"It is raining outside, so you can't wear what I would like you to wear."

"I'll check the weather and get back to you, but I will have a yellow fedora bucket hat on."

Part 2
Tahra

"We are now entering Downtown Crossing. Change here for the Orange and Green Line connections, and Red Line." Tahra exited the trolley and walked over to Orange Line. While waiting for Damien to arrive, she took the opportunity to use her spare time to inspect the Orange Line map that was on the subway wall and counted the number of stops before arriving at Charlestown. Just when she finished looking at the map, the brakes on the train came squealing so loud that she had no choice but to draw her attention to it.

Damien who was wearing a blue, yellow, and white jacket, was one the first of several passengers to step off the train; however, he came to a complete stop and directed his focus on the three gentlemen holding different musical instruments. Instead of walking toward him, she resisted and kept watching him from within the crowd. He appeared to be dazed by the music they are playing; however, she wondered what's it about this song. Does he find it so intriguing?

On nights like this, I wish
That raindrops would fall (yes, I do, hey baby, oh)
On nights like this, I wish
That raindrop would fall

While the band was still playing music, Damien unexpectedly spotted her out of the crowd. She watched him gait toward her, and with each step he took, it felt like, for her, his eyes were piercing through her life force. "You found me!" Tahra said as she came to embrace him.

"How can I find you if I never lost you," Damien said, but she said she was not buying it.

"How many girls have you told that?" she asked.

He replied, "Just you" and kissed her on the cheek. Immediately her cheeks began to flush hot with blood as she felt his lips softly caress her skin. "Come with me. I want to show you something."

He grabbed her arm and brought her to where the three musicians were standing. "This is one of my father's favorite songs." As the train arrived, she watched him pull out two dollars and some coins and then toss them into the guitar case on the floor.

"Thank you, my brother. You are like a pair of perfect verses over a tight beat." The musician in the middle said. She smiled back, thanking him, and Damien shook their hands.

"We are now entering Haymarket. Change here for the Green Line and MBTA."

Tahra held Damien's hand as they stepped off the train. She was astonished at how the walls, the benches, and the smell were still the same. "Taking it in?" he asked her.

"Absolutely! A lot of time has passed since I remember being on this side of town. However, as the saying goes, some things never change." After they departed from the escalator and arrived at the bus terminal, she released his hand. She twirled around while drenched in exuberant joy as her eyes gazed upon the North End's skyscrapers.

"I read somewhere…that happiness is only real when shared." She heard him say as she leaned into his arms. "Let's go. I can see our bus getting ready to turn into the bus terminal," he said to her, and she interlocked her hands with his. The sign on the approaching bus read "93 Sullivan." As they boarded the bus, he paid for both of their fares, and then they proceeded to sit at the back of the bus. At that moment, she felt secure; he had her back.

Part 3
Damien

Damien said, "I used to go to an elementary school not too far from here."

Tahra replied, "The Elliot?"

"Yeah. How did you know?" he asked.

"Before my grandmother passed, she used to live in Charlestown, and Elliot is the only school that I know of in the North End."

"Let me tell you a funny true story about destiny. When I was in the third grade, I got expelled from Harvard-Kent Elementary School for disobedience. However, later that year, my mother enrolled me in the Elliot. Eventually, I graduated from that school."

"So you're a terrible boy, hun?" she said

He explained, "No, I'm just a man willing to break the rules of society and regulations to succeed in life."

"Why?"

"Because it's in my nature. You won't understand, kid."

"Then help me understand."

"All in due time, my pretty."

She rested her head on his chest. "Then tell me the name of that song from Downtown Crossing the men were singing."

Damien smiled, and she smiled too. "'Nights Like This' by After 7. It's one of my father's favorite songs after my mother and he broke up.

Suddenly, the bus driver closed the doors, and Damien and Tahra stared out the window. After crossing several streetlights, he pointed to the beautiful and historical Custom House Tower. Despite it being constructed back in 1837, they were both astonished by the pristine condition of the skyscraper. As the bus continued to drive up North Washington Street, the city of North End's tall glass windows of the different buildings, the fast pace of other races of people that were walking from one place to another, and the unsettling traffic noise of cars and buses were slowly beginning to dissipate. And out of the blue, the old town of Boston's colonial architecture had finally emerged at center stage as if it was patiently waiting to reveal itself to them like flowers that bloom in the spring.

Damien watched in amazement at the beauty, and he looked at Tahra. "Can you believe that the structure of these buildings had not changed since the days of British colonial rule? The fact that it still stands today unblemished and unscathed for over two hundred years is what I consider timeless treasures."

Tahra looked into Damien's eyes." Yeah, I agree. It never gets old for me either. We Bostonians are pretty good at preserving the old. We both know that technology is a cause of our modern society, but we must subtly be aware of both the future as well as our past so that way we can see where we are heading. If needed, we can also remember where we came from," Tahra said as she directed his focus to the Boston Harbor by pointing to it.

From a distance, Damien could see, once he squinted, the three masts of the USS Constitution, also known as Old Ironsides, the world's oldest ship resting in the Navy Yard and surrounded by modern boats powered by gasoline. "Look how beautiful that is. Aren't they so beautiful?" Damien said as he was taken aback by the scenery of Boston Harbor along with its boats; it appeared that they had made an impression on him.

Part 5
Damien and Tahra

As the bus made a left turn onto Vine Street, Damien watched in suspense as he was excited to see the first school in his old neighborhood and the first school from which he got kicked out of in Charlestown. "That's the school." Damien pointed at the red brick building over to his left.

"Is this the school that sent you packing?" Tahra said while grinning.

"Well, it was doomed from the start—a permanent breakup," Damien said while inspecting the school campus.

"Come on. We're about to get off at the next stop." Damien pulled on the bell string to alert the bus driver to stop at the bus stop.

*****

Damien and Tahra exited the bus, and Damien pulled out the paper he had written Ms. Nolan's address on. He looked up at the pole to read the street's name, which matched what was on his paper: 1862 Monument Street. "This way," Damien said and took Tahra's hand as they crossed the street.

"What is the house number again?" asked Tahra.

"1862. She said it's before the Bunker Hill Monument. It's on the right-hand side," said Damien looking at the numbers on each house door.

"Oh, here it is!" said Tahra. Damien saw a layered brick build-ing covered with giant windows, and by the entrance to the door, colored in ruby red were two potteries, each sitting between the door.

"Wow, this is nice. I only passed by these houses heading to the library or the Boys and Girls Club. I've never been inside one," Damien said as he was fascinated by the house's exterior.

"Well, I've never been in houses like these either. Still, I heard that these houses were built back in the 1800s, but they look modern on the inside," Tahra said as she bent over to touch one of the plants.

Damien approached the door, but he turned to look at Tahra. "Oh yeah. I almost forgot to tell you."

Tahra's eyes grew wide. "What?" she replied.

"Ms. Nolan's significant other is a woman."

Chapter 8

One Nail Drive Out Another

Damien and Tahra

"It is so nice to meet you two! Let us get you two out of this rain. Come, come inside. Please, you can put your coats here on me coat stand," Ms. Nolan said, dressed in a green-gauze boatneck top and sky-blue jeans. Damien followed Tahra and then assisted her in removing her coat to place onto the free-standing coat rack. The hallway was attractive and well-lit with a solid oak floor and a center chandelier, and from the hallway, the stairwell led to the first floor.

"I love mahogany wood. Is this vintage, Ms. Nolan?" asked Tahra.

"Don't ever say that, my dear. She hates when people address her by her last name only. Ashling would do. She sort of cheeky like that loves to hear the sound of their name." Then, out of the blue, a tall, slender woman with hints of golden strains of hair color emerged from above the stairs wearing a red thermal top and blue denim jeans.

"I do not." Ashling smiled. "But this coat rack is vintage from me country. I had me ol' man send it to me long ago. Now every time me leave or come into me home, not for a moment is it possible for me not to reminisce of the lush green meadows covering the wonderful country hills of me home back on the island." Having made it to the top of the stairs, Ashling introduced us to her girlfriend, extending her hands toward Damien and Tahra. "This lovely lady here is Virginia Williams." Virginia shook their hands and kissed their cheeks. They followed both Ashling and Virginia into the living room. Tahra and Damien sat on a faux suede sofa, a decorative brick fireplace, and patio doors, which showcased the lovely Tobin bridge.

"You have a lovely home. Thank you both for inviting us," said Damien.

They all sat on the couch where Ashling said, "I had doubts."

He asked, "You did? But why?"

"Well, your bleeding father told me that you are involved with the bleeding church, and me thought nobody tried to stick their tongue in me ear with that silly nonsense," explained Ashling.

Tahra asked, "You're not open to many people, right?"

Virginia said, "Bloody hell, I almost got killed for trying to bring her to the pub last week. She is such a swot, but I love my little swot."

Ashling said, "Not true. She is talking a load of Barney. Anyway, your father reassured me, you know, to be sure, the kind of reassurance he promised me. I told him me would hear him out."

"Well, my father and I went to our usual fishing spot, where we relaxed by the reservoir and talked about life. I can speak freely to my father without worrying that I would get chastised. I told him that I had been questioning my faith ever since I was seven whether Jesus Christ is the only way for life after death to be possible. I have been hiding this secret for so long that I feel constant guilt. With no one to talk to and no one to explain my feelings to, in the end, I felt trapped. Does any of this make sense?" he said.

Virginia, Tahra, and Ashling all said yes at the same time.

Ashling exclaimed, "Pint off the black stuff for the mate, babe!"

Rubbish. He needs proper gin and tonic!" replied Virginia.

Damien gestured with his head as a sign of approval.

Ashling asked, "How you want it, mate?"

"On the rocks," he replied.

"Mmm, I sure needed that." Ashling started to shake her head. "Ah, nice one, but your father mustn't know about this."

Damien signaled that he had already sealed his mouth.

Everyone moved to the kitchen, where Virginia and Ashling had prepared shepherd's pie.

Virginia asked, "Does anyone care for a proper slice?"

Tahra and Damien both raised their hands.

"It was one of my favorite dishes when my grandmother used to make it," said Tahra.

Virginia said, "Sorry to hear about that. I didn't know she had passed."

She replied, "I'm afraid so. She passed away ten years ago from old age."

Tahra and Virginia shared a sad demeanor.

Virginia said, "Oh my god, I never meant to intrude, but I will tell you this: I can't promise it will taste like her cooking, but I haven't received any bloody complaints."

Both Virginia and Tahra cackled away.

*****

Ashling looked at Damien and said, "Do you fear death?"

Damien hesitated before he responded, "Have you heard of Pascal's wager?"

"I don't think so."

Both Tahra and Virginia listened carefully.

"If God exists, and we believe, we have an infinite gain (heaven). If God exists, and we don't believe that, then we have the potential of an infinite loss (hell, or at least eternal separation from God). If God does NOT EXIST, and we believe that God exists, we lose nothing. If God does NOT EXIST, and we believe that God doesn't exist, we essentially gain nothing."

Ashling seemed puzzled, and Virginia and Tahra stared at each other. "Which one do you believe in, Damien?" said Tahra.

"First, I don't fear death, and second, I have three questions that I would ask: Where do we come from? What is our purpose? And what happens when we die? Third, if I was to believe in Jesus Christ, then I can't live a life of pleasure. I wouldn't be able to live a life of my own free will without consequences. I'm free-spirited and love to take risks. In my opinion, to live as a Christian requires having the character of Christ. Which is a lifestyle that no one can replicate except Christ, in my opinion."

Virginia handed out the shepherd's pie to everyone except Damien, who waived it off. "Does your shepherd's pie contain any meat?" Everyone stared at Damien.

"Are you a vegetarian?" asked Tahra.

"No, I'm a pescatarian." Feeling relieved, Virginia exhaled.

"May I offer you some salmon and rice?" Damien quickly said yes. "What about you? Do you believe in Jesus Christ, Tahra?" Tahra took a bite of shepherd's pie before she answered.

"I don't know. I can't believe in something that I believe to be mystic, but I do believe in the stars and the universe, but if there's a mastermind out there, a master creator of some sort, then I await to see him, to see her, or to see it. What about you? Do you have faith in Jesus Christ?" They all looked at Virginia to see what she would say.

"They say faith is belief without evidence and reason. Well, it's safe to say that's also the definition of delusion. When I was a little girl, I remember my grandmother had died, and my parents reassured me that it was bloody okay because my grandmother was now in a better place (heaven). However, I can't see heaven, nor can my parents, so why lie? Was it to keep me from being sad or angry? Children can figure out when you're lying to them." Damien and the others nodded their heads in agreement.

Damien took a bite of his salmon. "What about you, Ashling? Where does your faith lie?" Ashling steadily rocked the chair she was sitting in.

"Well, me parents never accepted me for what I am, you know. That was a big problem, you know, and still is, but your father came through for the young wan. I reckon, your father and I met in the first year back in high school, where I was the biggest tomboy, Christ's sake. I told your father that I like girls, but he didn't care. He said he just wanted to be my friend. I told him, 'You want to be friends?' and he said, 'Yeah.' I told him my parents wanted to start seeing me around some young lads, and then he wouldn't believe it. Your father proposed an insane idea to me. Whenever they come around, we could pretend to be dating, crazy, hun? Anyway, our scheme of things went on throughout high school, and when we graduated, we both became so close we were unwilling to separate, and it's how your father and I became a couple. Bloody hell. It seemed like yesterday. It has been a fantastic romance your father and I shared, but all good things must end."

We were rudely interrupted by the loud thunderstorm. "*Ashling.* Such a beautiful name. What does it mean?"

Ashling crossed her legs and put both hands on her lap. "I think it means to dream or to vision. My dad was the one who gave me that name. He said that it originated from a poet lamenting over her people's hardship."

Ashling was taken aback by the question. "You love your father?"

Ashling smiled. "I do, and I miss him still. Next month, he would've turned seventy-two." Immediately, Ashling's blue gaze met Damien, and it quickly faded.

The wind was blowing hard, the clouds were getting dark, and Damien was in deep thought. "How did you and Tahra meet?" Tahra looked over at me with a blissful look.

"Well, I skipped church that day because my head felt heavy. Somehow, someway I ended up at Brilliance and Creativity Museum, where I met Tahra. We shared a great conversation. I didn't want to leave without seeing her again, as it was time to go."

Tahra blushed hard. "And I gave him Doctor Jean Dubois brochure," replied Tahra.

Damien and Tahra both laughed. "So nice you two are getting along now. Oh well! How ya getting on?" asked Ashling.

Tahra had looked at Damien, confused. "I don't follow. What is she talking about, Damien?" said Tahra, upset and confused. "Damien, Damien." Tahra got up and walked downstairs and grabbed her coat off the stand.

"I'm so sorry. I didn't mean to get you in trouble," said Ashling.

"Don't worry. Did my dad tell you about another girl named Yemaya?" he asked in a whisper.

"Oh, bloody hell. Damien, is there anything we can do?" said Virginia.

"No, there's not, but thank you for inviting us over. Bye, Ashling and Virginia." Damien rushed downstairs and got his coat before he exited. He could see Tahra downhill by the corner, waiting for the bus. "Hey, hey, Tahra. Wait up. Let me explain," Damien said, trying to reason with her, but it was futile.

"Leave me the fuck alone," replied Tahra.

CHAPTER 9

We Must Go Backward to Move Forward

Part 1
Damien

Damien woke up to the sound of birds chirping, then looked at the time, and it read 8:27 a.m. His mom must be cooking breakfast because he could hear her, but before he would eat, he should wash up first. He walked over to the window and wondered how Tahra was doing. It got intense yesterday. Damien never saw her blow a gasket like that. That was it. Once again, he found a way to ruin a good thing. There was nothing he could say that would improve the situation, absolutely nothing. Damien slowly walked toward the window. He thought about when he was in third grade when he had been hit by a tractor-trailer while trying to cross the street at the Navy Yard in Charlestown. When he woke from the coma, he saw his mother and sister sitting by his side, tired. The petrified look on their faces reminded Damien of how much he meant to them.

Part 2
Damien and His Family

"I didn't think you were coming down. Grab yourself a plate. Food is about to be served," said his mom.

"Mom, we need to talk about a crucial matter," Damien said, dismayed, but before he could utter a word, his sister intruded into the kitchen.

"What's up, big bro? Are you feeling alright? You seemed kinda tired," she said as she made her way to the fridge.

"You all, please come to the table so I can say what I have been holding back." Damien was trembling but knew he had to go through with it if he wanted to be free from this.

"Hunny, why are you shaking?" His mother could see Damien sweating profusely around his face and neck.

"Bro, did you kill somebody?" Damien became enraged by his sister's comment that with one look at her, she quickly apologized.

"I have been keeping something from you and the church for a long time. If I hide it any longer, I might lose myself or, worse, go insane. But I'm tired, tired of living a fraudulent life, tired of socializing with church members and feeling guilty about it. Do you know how it feels to hide behind a mask? I walk around every day and every night disguised as someone else. Ask me then, why I do it. And my response would be that I don't want to see my mother cry. I wouldn't dare offset my burden for her sake. She doesn't deserve it. However, what am I supposed to do? Am I supposed to accept the inevitable impending hardship and endure the resulting pain with fortitude? Shall I go on and on and accept the utmost unpleasant fact? That I hate putting people's needs first and my needs second. Look, I know the both of you have cared for me tremendously, but it's time for me to sever ties with the church." Mother was sobbing, and Damien went to comfort her.

"Don't cry, Mom. My intentions are not to hurt you. Remember, Mom, when you found out I was getting beat up by the neighborhood bully? Do you remember what you did, a disdain I unfortunately remember? I tried and lost. There was no way that I could argue my way out of this. You had brought me to the boy's apartment and sat down with his mother and reconciled the matter. But you know what moral lesson I took from that experience? A mother's love is like nothing else in this world." Damien watched closely as his mother shed even more tears. He kissed her on the cheek while reassuring her that everything will be fine.

His mom wiped her tears and glared at Damien with pain. "You know that all ever wanted for you and your sister was for you to have each other, to protect each other from the evil of this world is all that I ever wanted. But you, Damien, always had to be the free spirit, the one who cannot be restrained or tied down, and the one who never possesses the ability to follow the traditional path." She sighed for a second before she could continue. "They told me it was a phase all young adults go through, but I would eventually grow out of it. As time went on, I sat back and watched you become the man of God or at least partially." She grabbed onto my sister's arm. "Whatever you feel like doing now is fine with me. Whatever direction you must take to feel completely free, then you have my support and love." Feeling intoxicated by this blissful moment, he imagined that we all needed more of this.

Part 3
Damien and His Sister

Now in the living room, Damien was relaxing with his sister, and his mom went to rest in her room. "So you don't believe in Jesus Christ anymore?" Damien's sister asked. She sounded very concerned.

"What made you think that I ever did?" She shrugged her shoulders in a gesture that she didn't know why.

"If he is real, then you won't be able to join us in paradise. You do not want to get left behind, do you?" She stared at Damien, awaiting an answer, but Damien seated calmly at the edge of the couch.

"Sure, I want to see all of you again. I would love for that to happen, but I believe there's more than one way to get to paradise. If I'm wrong, I will make the most of my time with you." He stared off into the distance trees right outside the living room's window.

"How do you think the church is going to take it? What about the choir?"

Damien slowly inhaled, and then he exhaled. "I'm tired of lying. Now it's time for me to be honest—honest about who I am and honest about what I believe regarding where I stand. The best way to confront the church is to be honest and lay out everything." His sister looked at him as if she saw a ghost.

"What about Yemaya?" she asked, but Damien continued to stare off into the distance.

CHAPTER 10

Fix You

Part 1
Damien

As light rain began to fall, the church members pulled out their umbrellas to get out of the shower and advance to the front. The parking lot was packed with cars trying to find a parking space. It felt like Damien was in a circus with people hunkering their horns trying to get inside to park. Meanwhile, everyone who could pass as aunts and uncles, as grandparents, as partners, and also as parents were making their way to the entrance.

Damien's sister was holding his hand while his mom slowly walked behind them. On their way up, he noticed a young boy telling the woman holding his hand that he didn't want to go to church. Then at that very moment, Damien remembered when he was a young boy who argued with his mother. He let his mind wander for a few seconds until he felt a slight yank on my left hand.

The door opened, and a statue of the cross hung on the wall for all to see. Damien immediately took a look at his sister, and she winked at him. As everyone welcomed new guests and current members, he told his sister they would meet in the auditorium. His mother had asked Damien where he was going, but before he could answer, the pastor's wife greeted her. He made a beeline to the men's bathroom to think about what I was going to say.

"Bro, where have you been?" It was Sky dressed up like he was attending a prom.

"I needed time to reflect, but whatever you hear from me, understand that you're my brother. Okay?" Sky could see Damien was serious, so rather than be nosy, he left it at that and nodded his head.

People are chatting away while trying to find their way to their seats; however, their children were playing with other children and laughing while their parents were escorting them back to the children's area. Meanwhile, as Damien casually scrolled up and down the aisle with his eyes, he saw Yamaya enter the doors with her mother and father. I couldn't lie, but every time he glanced at her, he got moonstruck again.

They made haste to their seats, but they got interrupted by Ms. Franklin's family. While her parents were socializing, Yemaya would look in Damien's direction now and then, and they would communicate with their eyes. Damien wanted to know why, but the words just got lost in translation.

The service was about to begin, and the pastor started by saying, "How is everyone today? Well, GOD that we serve is living, not dead. Can I get an amen? Today, I will preach about the sermon on Mont and, more importantly, why prayer is so important. We all have different challenges, which we all can equate to other kinds of stress. In those circumstances, we all could use a little help. Don't you agree? That's why we all need to give our baggage to the true GOD, who listens to our pain, heart, and prayer. Now if we turned to Matthew 7:7–8, let us read what our Lord says. 'Ask, and it will be given to you. Seek, and you will find. Knock, and the door will be opened. For everyone who asks receives, the one who seeks finds, and to the one who knocks, the door will be opened.' Is anyone feeling tired, anyone feeling depressed, or anyone feeling like they need to talk to someone? Come down the aisle and seek GOD, and he will open your door for you. Hallelujah, yes, Lord. Please answer all our prayers, and we thank you, in the name of Jesus Christ, amen."

Part 2
Damien and the Pastor

Some people were leaving, while others were enjoying their conversation with the nun and church members, and some were not ready to leave yet. Currently, Damien's mother was making herself occupied with Sister Mary and the pastor's wife laughing hysterically at a joke Sister Mary made.

Damien managed to slip out of the auditorium to go and see the pastor in his chamber. He knocked on the door several times and waited to enter the pastor's chamber. He pushed through the door using more strength than anticipated, and then one of the sisters of the church appeared standing behind the pastor's desk. She said the pastor would be right with him and then offered me to seat on this lovely sofa that felt very soft when I sat on it. She then disappeared through the door and into the hallway.

Damien took this time to study the pastor's accolades that seemed to decorate his walls. He graduated from Boston College, where he obtained his master of theology, and from Boston University, where he received his religious and theological studies. Staring at the many books that were on his bookshelf, Damien assumed the pastor must've kept the books that he had studied. Also, there was a medium-sized picture of the pastor and his wife standing next to a Basilica. Damien thought that was pretty.

Suddenly, the doors opened, and the pastor made his way in. "Hi. I'm surprised to see you here. Is everything okay?" Damien watched the pastor move into his space.

"Well, Pastor, I admire your work and must admit they're mighty achievements." The pastor seemed flattered.

"Yes, it took a while, but with the Lord, all things are possible. You see that picture with me and my wife?" Damien looked at the picture of the pastor with his wife; they seemed so happy.

"You two look blissful in this picture. Where was it taken?"

The pastor was caught off guard examining the picture as if he was looking for the very first time. "It never gets old, but that is our honeymoon picture in Italy. The first time she had been on a plane.

My blood must've stopped circulating in my left hand because she was squeezing so tight! Okay, that's enough talking about me because I know you didn't want to come to talk to me about that."

Damien chuckled. "I wanted to tell you that I enjoyed Sunday service, and I understand why people, in their way, seek help from Jesus Christ. They would like to connect with him, but I'm afraid the connection between Jesus and I is no more. Let me be honest with you, Pastor. Ever since I was a young boy, I always wonder about life after death. Call it a fixation, but I always wanted to know what next. Do I have to believe in Jesus to find out, and why do I have to believe in Christ to see my loved ones in paradise? Call me crazy, but I strongly believe there's another way, and I'm willing to take that chance even though it may cost me my eternal life."

The pastor sat right next to me and began to sigh.

Damien continued, "I talked to my family about it, and they respected my decision. If I'm wrong, then I would make sure to have the best life with my family here on earth."

The pastor was thinking hard. "Your mother came to me when you were just a little boy with concerns about you questioning a life after death. I figured putting you into Bible study would help, yet it only made you want to question more. Son, I don't think I have the answer you're looking for. However, the Bible says,

> A new heaven and a new earth, for the first heaven and the first earth had passed away, and there was no longer any sea. I saw the Holy City, the new Jerusalem, coming down out of heaven from God, prepared as a bride beautifully dressed for her husband. And I heard a loud voice from the throne saying, "Look! God's dwelling place is now among the people, and he will dwell with them. They will be his people, and God himself will be with them and be their God." He will wipe every tear from their eyes. There will be no more death or mourning or crying or pain, for the old order of things has passed away.

"That is the word of God, and the word of God is truth."

Damien stared through the window and thought heavily about what the pastor had said; he had heard that same scripture repeated over and over to him in bible study.

"Damien, I appreciate you stopping by to see me. May God bless you."

Part 3
Damien and Yemaya

As Damien was heading to the exit, he could see that almost everyone left the church. Sister Madeleine thanked him for coming by before he departed through the doors. Once he stepped outside, the whole club was waiting for me. "You in trouble? We saw you went into the pastor's chambers. Is everything alright?" asked Sky.

"I want to tell you all something, and it is about me being in the choir. I will be leaving the church just until I feel ready to come back." They were freaking out, except Yemaya. "You can reach me anytime so don't worry.

"Is it something we did?" asked Sky and Mary Alice.

"No, we always will remain the best of friends." Damien embraced them while holding back the tears. "Can I talk to you?" Damien asked Yemaya, and she nodded her head. Damien took her hand, and they headed over to the park.

"I want to say that I'm not mad at you. You were trying to protect me." Yemaya couldn't refrain from crying.

"Come here. Why are you crying?" replied Damien, but she continued to cry. "You did it because you care about me and you didn't want to lose me." She nodded her head to confirm that was true. "Today's message that the pastor spoke of opened my eyes to how the world can use Jesus."

Yemaya's eyes grew wide. "In what way?" she asked.

"Connection is important for people to have. Whether they believe or not, it's important for Jesus that people at least try to reach out to him." She smiled and tried to kiss him, but Damien put his two fingers together and pushed them softly against her lips. "Maybe we should take a break to find out if this is the correct path for us, you know." She looked at him in the eye, and a tear fell.

"What will you do now?" Yemaya asked.

"I'm going to allow my imagination to run wild." Yemaya put her soft hands on his cheeks and kissed them, for she knew she would never seem again.

Part 4
Damien and Tahra

As Damien opened the door for the young couples, he made his way through the door and saw one of the employees at the information desk. "Hello, is the Tahra here, please?" The young girl sighed.

"She doesn't want to talk to you! You should go home because you're only wasting your time." Before he could respond, he saw Tahra coming out of the break room.

"Tahra, I know you probably don't want to see me again, but please give me ten minutes." She looked at her friend.

"I tried to explain to him, but he wouldn't take no for an answer. You want me to call security?"

Tahra gestured at her and said no. "You have ten minutes, and then I'm gone." Damien nodded.

They step outside to get more privacy, and the couple made their way to the front door. Tahra was signaling her watch. "You know, I went to church today, and all I could think about was you, but I know that's not an excuse for lying to you. I never meant to hurt you, and I don't want to because you mean the whole world to me, Tahra. I don't want anyone else because you are the only person I want."

She shook her head. "You don't want me. You don't know what you want," she said as she looked off into a far distance.

Damien caressed her arm and then gently touched her face, and then softly kissed her. "Baby, you're all I want."

She looked at him, not able to fight the tears. "You better not hurt me, Damien."

Damien pulled her close to his chest and kissed her forehead. "I promise, baby." They sat on the bench looking at different people kayaking in the Charles River.

ABOUT THE AUTHOR

David Vilfrance is a writer, an author, a fisherman, and a home renovator. He is an adventurous kind of spirit who is always looking for the next big thing.

www.ingramcontent.com/pod-product-compliance
Lightning Source LLC
Chambersburg PA
CBHW022036150726

47990CB00002B/986